GW00391798

Mine to Keep

(The prequel to *The Butterfly Storm*)

by

KATE FROST

LEMON TREE PRESS

Paperback Edition 2018

ISBN 978-0-9954780-4-6

Copyright © Kate Frost 2018

This novel is entirely a work of fiction. The names, characters and incidents portrayed in it are the product of the author's imagination. Any resemblance to actual persons, living or dead, or events or localities is entirely coincidental.

The moral right of Kate Frost to be identified as the author of this work has been asserted by her in accordance with the Copyright, Designs and Patents Act of 1988.

All rights reserved in all media. No part of this publication may be reproduced, stored in a retrieval system, or transmitted, in any form, or by any means, electronic, mechanical, photocopying, recording or otherwise, without the prior written permission of the author and/or publisher.

Cover design by Jessica Bell.

Mine to Keep

by

KATE FROST

LEMON
TREE
PRESS

Books in *The Butterfly Storm* Series

Mine to Keep
The Butterfly Storm
The Birdsong Promise

For Soula and my Greek family

Chapter One

Grey light spills into the kitchen, accentuating the dirt patterns on the outside of the window. This early on a Saturday morning, the road outside is quiet, with only an occasional car passing by. The flat is unusually quiet too, but then I'm never up this early on a weekend and my housemates are still in bed after a late night out. I tuck my feet up on the windowsill ledge and sip my tea. Dirty plates and cups clutter the work surface and overflow in the sink. Empty kebab trays are scattered across the wooden kitchen table and I presume that Lucy and Jess brought their boyfriends home with them last night. At least the state of the flat is not my problem for the next seven days.

A car beeps. I glance across the road to where a taxi has pulled up outside the newsagent opposite. I down the rest of my tea, grab my bag and jacket from the back of one of the kitchen chairs and make my way downstairs to my suitcase by the front door. A pile of post for the downstairs flat spills across the narrow shelf and a bike, which constantly gets in everyone's way, leans against the peeling cream paint of the hall wall. I sigh and remind myself that none of this is going to annoy me for a week at least. Goodbye, lazy housemates, mess and work; hello, Cephalonia, sun, sea, relaxation and whatever else takes our fancy.

My best friend, Candy, greets me with a squeal and a hug and the taxi driver heaves my suitcase into the boot. Then we're off, hurtling through empty Bristol streets to the coach station, the aftermath of Friday night evident in the litter overflowing from bins and strewn across pavements and young men looking the worse for wear staggering through the city centre. The sky is an ominous grey despite it being the end of May.

Candy is dressed for Greece in a short white flared skirt that stops just above her tanned knees, jewelled sandals, a sunny yellow top and a denim jacket thrown effortlessly over the top. I'm not so optimistic in jeans, a long-sleeved tunic top and faded blue canvas trainers, but Candy's always been effortlessly cool ever since we first met at school at eleven years-old.

Despite being bleary eyed from a long coach journey we squeeze each other's hands in excitement when we reach the airport, and I realise how much I'm looking forward to time away – time out of my life. An uncomplicated few days sunbathing, drinking and eating with my best friend.

I have a seat by the window on the plane, with Candy in the middle one next to me and a young couple separated by the aisle next to her. I contemplate doing the decent thing and swapping seats with them but figure they have a whole lifetime to get loved up. I don't spend nearly enough time with Candy any more with her working long hours, me trudging through the deathly 9 to 5, and various boyfriends over the years reducing the free time we have to simply be friends.

A trickle of air filters through from above me and I settle back into my seat with the satisfaction that our holiday has really started.

'I'm so excited,' Candy says with a grin as she tucks her shoulder bag beneath the seat in front of her, clips her belt together and rests her head back on the seat. 'The last time we did this we were twenty-one. Three years ago. How did we miss our yearly girlie holiday?'

'Boyfriends,' I say. 'One of us has always been with someone – you more than me I should add – but there's either not been the time or we were going on holiday with someone else.'

'Boys.' Candy wrinkles her nose. 'It's so much nicer having a holiday with a girl – no dirty socks left by the side of the bed or wet swimming trunks dripping on the bathroom floor.'

'I promise I'll behave myself.' I wink. Candy's always been a girlie girl and me more of a tomboy, although that's changed a bit over the years as I've embraced skirts, dresses and now feel naked without my nails painted. I still feel a mess next to Candy though, my red hair tangled from the wind – and I didn't bother with a full face of make-up that early in the morning. One day I'll learn to be effortlessly cool…

'I'm looking forward to a few men-free days in the sun,' Candy says as the plane begins to taxi to the runway.

'Speak for yourself.' I grip the armrests of my seat as the plane roars forward along the runway until we're in the air, heading higher and higher through the grey clouds blanketing the city. I turn to Candy. 'Unlike you, my life is man-free and has been for way too long.'

It's late afternoon in Greece by the time our plane begins its descent to Cephalonia International Airport. The charcoal skies back home have been left behind, and now the sky is a deep blue, peppered with specks of white cloud. The sea below us glistens in the sunshine.

The difference in temperature is obvious the moment we step from the plane – we've kissed goodbye to the dull but humid morning in Bristol and the warmth of the Mediterranean sun embraces us. Candy is dressed for the climate; I should have worn less.

The island charms me as much as our cheerful taxi driver does – he's a head shorter than us and rounder with greying stubble but his smile is welcoming. He chews gum constantly and keeps hold of a string of beads wrapped around his right hand the whole time he drives.

'You come here before?' he asks in a thick Greek accent as he pulls out of the airport.

'First time,' Candy says, clicking her seatbelt in as we pick up speed. 'Although I've been to Rhodes before.'

'Ah, *kala*, it nice but not nice like Cephalonia. You stay long?'

I lean forward and look out of the window. 'Just a week.'

'Can you recommend where we should go? The best beaches?' Candy asks. 'We know Myrtos is supposed to be amazing.'

'It is,' the taxi driver says. '*Ala*, it full of tourists, not so bad now early in season, but still many, many people. You go on boat trip to the other islands, not busy, quiet beaches, the best. I give you name of boat hire places – not expensive.'

The island passes by in a blur – we glimpse snatches of deep blue sea as we wind our way along the coast road before we head inland the hour and a half to Fiskardo in the north. A radio station is on in the background playing what I think of as typically Greek songs that make me tap my feet. As we pass a small church at the side of the road, the taxi driver draws a cross down his chest and kisses the beads clutched in his hand. Without having even properly set foot on the island, I already feel fully immersed in Greek life.

Candy was adamant that our days of finding the cheapest hotel room possible are over, so we've splashed out.

'We've both got good jobs,' she'd argued when I'd balked at the price of Hotel Kalokairi. She'd quickly worn me down with the photos of a stunning twin room with a spacious balcony with sea views and a swimming pool set in landscaped gardens. It's not like we do this often and we deserve it, we work hard – my job as a designer in an advertising agency is going well even if it's not what I want to do, and last year Candy landed herself a dream job working as a make-up artist on *Casualty*.

In reality our room exceeds my expectations; the photos I'd seen don't do it justice – it's brighter, more spacious and there are lovely touches like a vase of white roses on the coffee table between two armchairs that face the balcony and the inviting blue of the Ionian Sea.

'Nice,' Candy says as she hands euros to the guy who

brought our bags up to the room. He leaves us with a 'thank you' and a wink.

I unzip my suitcase and pull out T-shirts, vest tops and shorts. I hang my dress and cropped trousers in the wardrobe. 'Do you remember our last holiday to Spain?'

'Are you kidding? Maybe that's the real reason we've left it so long to go on holiday together again.' She lounges back on to the bed nearest the balcony and stretches out. 'Definitely no thin and lumpy mattress here and at least we don't have to share a bed this time.'

I go over to the mini bar and pour a generous amount of Malibu into two glasses and top it up with Coke. I hand one to Candy. 'Do you remember the colour of the water that came out of the taps in our room?'

Candy gags. 'We were very young and poor at the time.'

'Well, this time you chose well,' I clink my glass against hers. 'To the best week ever.'

Chapter Two

I wake to daylight streaming through the open balcony doors and it takes me a moment to remember where I am. I shuffle until I'm propped up against the pillows; I can see a patch of blue through the balcony railings, and Candy's tanned legs and bare feet resting on an empty chair. I've already forgotten what day it is – Sunday I think, but I guess every day this week is going to feel like it's the weekend. I yawn, stretch and swing my legs out of bed and pad across the cool tiled floor and out on to the balcony.

'How long have you been up?' I rub my eyes and squint at how bright it is outside.

'A while,' she says. 'I'm conditioned to waking up for 7am or earlier call times.'

I grunt, my head still in a sleep haze. 'I don't know how you do it – a 9 o'clock start is early enough for me. Weekends and holidays are for sleeping in.'

Candy swings her feet off the chair and I sit down. 'What do you fancy doing today?'

'I think we should explore Fiskardo. Take it easy, do a bit of shopping, relax by the pool.'

'Sounds good to me.'

We have breakfast on one of the tables on the patio above the pool. The hotel doesn't feel crowded with just a few couples and groups of friends filling some of the tables. Bougainvillea spill from large clay pots on either side of the patio, splashing deep green and purple against the white walls, and pale pink roses entwine through the railings. White umbrellas shade the wooden sunloungers dotted around the pool, bright against the deep blue sky above us. Each lounger has a dark blue towel rolled up on it and a selection of fresh fruit in a bowl on the low table next to it. I sigh at the thought of the holidays Candy and I had in the past where we missed out on this kind of luxury.

A feast is laid in front of us: watermelon and pineapple slices, croissants, ham, cheeses, and filo squares filled with either cream or cheese that the waitress serving us calls *bougatsa*. Whatever they're called, they're delicious and we polish off the lot. I sip my coffee and lean back in my chair, my stomach full. I'll worry about how many calories I've eaten when I get back to the UK. The next few days are all about indulging.

We need to walk off breakfast before we can even contemplate a dip in the pool and a cocktail. Candy is wearing a new sundress that she bought especially for our holiday and I'm in a colourful maxi dress that I never got the chance to wear the summer before because we never really had a summer in the UK.

Our hotel is in a perfect position towards one end of the candy-coloured Venetian buildings that line Fiskardo's waterfront, yet only a short walk from the hub of activity in the centre of the town with bustling cafés and gorgeous little shops selling everything from pottery to local wine. I buy a straw hat in a cute boutique shop set back from the harbourside and we browse a stall by the harbour selling jewellery.

'*Kalimera*,' the lady behind the stall says.

'*Kalimera*,' we chorus in reply.

'You like souvenir of your holiday?' the lady asks, running her hand across the rings, bracelets, earrings and necklaces displayed in front of us.

'You made these yourself?' Candy asks, picking up a necklace strung with tiny shells. 'They're beautiful.'

The lady nods and smiles. 'Thank you.'

Candy turns the necklace in her hands and holds it up to the sunlight. 'How much?'

'Twenty-five euros.'

'Ah okay, I'll think about it.' Candy places the necklace back and with a smile we head down to the waterfront where the bars and cafés are beginning to fill up with people cooling down with drinks or stopping for an early lunch.

'Shall we get a drink somewhere?' I stop and gaze at the cream and dusky pink buildings with their deep green and sky blue shutters, unsure how we're going to choose a place when everywhere makes me want to pull up a chair and order a beer.

Candy touches my arm. 'Wait here a minute; I'm going back for that necklace.'

She spins round and walks back to the stall selling the handmade jewellery. I move out of the way of the people walking along the waterfront and stand at the edge of the harbour. It's a perfect morning with sunshine warming my bare shoulders and just enough breeze to feel comfortable. The sky looks like it's been painted on without a wisp of cloud to break up the deep blue. Boats line the harbour and I think how lovely it would be to set sail, out into the calm water of the Ionian Sea like the tourists waiting to board the largest boat in the harbour. I wonder where they'll be sailing to? A deserted beach on Cephalonia? The island of Ithaca just across the bay that we can see from our hotel room? My eyes drift past the couples in their shorts and flip-flops to the next sailing boat. *Artemis* is painted in gold on the side and on the deck a dark-haired man in his twenties throws a rope to a crew member before picking another one up and neatly coiling it. I glance back to where Candy is looking like she's bartering over the necklace she'd seen. I wander a little further down the harbour towards the boats. The man has shorts slung low on his waist and his chest and feet are bare. Even from this far away I can see his chest muscles as he pulls at the rope.

'What you up to?' Candy joins me on the edge of the harbourside.

'Admiring the view,' I say, nodding towards *Artemis* where the topless guy has sat down on the deck and cracked open a bottle of Coke.

Candy follows my gaze across the harbour and snorts. 'I bet you were.'

'Did you buy it?' I drag my eyes away from the boat and Candy holds up the shell necklace.

'There's a really nice looking café close to where I got this. Come on, I'm parched.' She hooks her arm in mine and drags me away from the harbour, back into the throng of tourists. The café is on the seafront, with tables scattered on the pavement and an awning providing shade. We choose a free table right at the edge overlooking the harbour, and order. Our frappés arrive with a complimentary plate of crumbly biscuits. I take a sip of the cold sweet coffee and sit back in my seat, sighing.

'This is the life,' I say. This is what I've wanted for so long, to stop for a few days, to halt the constant routine of work. It's been almost four years already since I graduated from university and although I'm using my illustration degree it's not in the way I want; it's not the job I saw myself in or want to stay in long term.

'You know, his friend's cute too,' Candy says, leaning forwards and pulling her sunglasses down to the end of her nose to get a better look. I'm so wrapped up in my thoughts it takes me a moment to realise that she's talking about the men on the boat. She pushes her sunglasses firmly back in place. 'But I'm done with holiday romances.'

'Anyway, aren't you with Paul?' I take a sip of my frappé and gaze across to the boat.

'Um, sort of. But it's not going anywhere. I've kinda known for ages that it's over, we just need to properly break up.' Candy places her tanned hand on my pale arm. 'You know, you could always go over and say hi. Or *yasou*.'

Candy's nails are long and bubblegum pink. I tuck my hands around my glass. My nails are neat but short and painted a deep purple-black. They're chipped at the edges. 'No way am I walking over there. They might not even speak

English.'

'Everyone speaks English here.' She takes her Greek phrase book from out of her bag that's hooked over the back of her chair and flicks through it. She stops at a page and smiles. 'Or you could say this. *Boro na se keraso ena poto?*'

'What does that mean?'

'Can I buy you a drink?'

'I'm not saying that because I'm not going over there.'

'Fancy a shag would probably work too.'

I slap her arm and she laughs and takes a bite of biscuit.

'Ah well,' she says waving one hand in front of us and pushing crumbs into her mouth with the other. 'We have a good view from here, at least until they set sail with a boatload of hot girls and you lose your chance of talking to him forever.'

It is a good view, even without the bonus of the two Greeks on *Artemis*. We have a perfect spot on one of the central cafés on the harbourside overlooking the clear blue Ionian Sea. We'd left behind clouds, rain and work in the UK for blue skies and a slice of luxury for a week. I close my eyes and tilt my head, allowing the warmth of the sun to caress my face. There's background chatter from the surrounding tables, mostly a mix of Greek and English; the clink of glasses and cutlery on plates and the smell of meat being cooked over a hot grill.

I open my eyes and let them rest again on the taller dark-haired Greek on the boat – the one who'd first caught my eye. Every time he moves or lifts something his muscles tense, shown off to perfection by his deep tan.

'You can't stop looking at him, can you?' Candy says.

I force my eyes away from the boat. 'I've been single for too long, that's all.'

'We should do something about that this evening – have a proper night out.'

'I thought you wanted this to be a man-free holiday?'

Candy shrugs. 'No harm in looking.'

After an afternoon spent exploring the rest of the town and

then a couple of hours sunbathing by the hotel pool, we head back to our room and take it in turns to have a shower, then crack open a bottle of wine while we're getting ready. I don't redo my nails, just paint over them. My face at least is sun-kissed and I use a light fake tan so I'm not completely pale against Candy.

As we walk along the harbourside to where Fiskardo comes alive with its bars and restaurants, I realise what I love about the Mediterranean lifestyle – how laid back it is, people out to enjoy themselves rather than on a mission to get drunk. Back home the centre of the city ends up being littered with paralytic teenagers and twenty-somethings by the early hours after a night out. Not my kind of fun any longer. I seem to have grown out of getting wasted.

We eat at a fish restaurant by the waterfront and devour fried mussels and calamari, alongside the salty freshness of a Greek salad, all washed down with sweet red wine. The stresses of everyday life back home fade away as I knock my glass against Candy's.

'Cheers,' she says. 'Or should we say, *yamas*!'

'*Yamas*!' I take a sip of my wine and skewer an olive with my fork. 'This was a good choice.'

'What, this restaurant?'

'That too but I meant coming here, to Cephalonia.'

'I've always wanted to come to this island,' Candy says, grinning across our candlelit table. 'Ever since Martha at work went here on her honeymoon. You know how sometimes you get fed up of hearing people bang on about how amazing their holiday was, but even though she talked about it a lot – and I mean a lot – she just made me want to visit. I know it's supposed to be completely touristy but we have to go to Myrtos beach, even if it's just to take a photo.'

'I thought it's quite a drive away?'

'Uh huh,' Candy nods. 'We should hire a car, go to Myrtos tomorrow and then we can drive ourselves back to the airport at the end of the week – save ourselves a fortune in taxi fare. I don't mind driving; I've driven in Spain before.'

'Okay, let's do it.' I clink my glass against hers.

Candy smiles and gulps a mouthful of wine. Behind her the darkness is broken up by the lights from fishing boats far out in the bay. Beyond that a cluster of tiny silver lights show where the sea ends and the island of Ithaca begins.

'You know, I've been thinking, maybe we should move in together.' Candy swirls her wine around her glass and looks across the table at me with her eyebrows raised. 'What do you think?'

I laugh. 'I feel like you've just proposed and I don't know what to say.'

'Charming!' She puts her wine down on the white tablecloth and leans forward. 'What I mean is, if I hadn't gone to live in London straight from uni and had come back to Bristol, then we'd have shared a flat together, wouldn't we?'

'Definitely.'

'I know you get on fine with your housemates, and I do too with mine, but it'd be nice to spend more time with you. Sharing a flat would be the perfect answer. Think about it – we don't have to decide anything now, it's just a thought.'

I squeeze lemon over the remaining mussels and pop one in my mouth. 'I think my mum's still pissed that I moved in with Lucy and Jess after uni instead of with her.'

'Well, she should have thought about the impact lying to you for years about your father would have. I've always loved your mum but I have no sympathy for her dropping a bombshell on you like that.'

The toe-tapping Greek music washes towards us from further down the waterfront with the clink of glasses and knives and forks on plates. A man at the table behind us booms something in Greek and a barrage of replies drown out my thoughts for a moment. I love the mix of Greeks and tourists – it makes the place feel authentic and real.

'I think Mum was mostly pissed that she lost me as her pulling partner just as I got to the age where it was kind of okay to go out on the pull with her daughter.'

'Is it really ever okay for a mum and daughter to go out on the pull?'

'No, you're right, it isn't, but then me and Mum never had

a normal mother daughter relationship did we? Anyway, you know from the times Mum came out with us it was me looking out for her and making sure she didn't get up to no good, rather than the other way round.'

Candy sighs and leans back in her chair. 'Those were the days.' She sticks her fork into one of the mussels, puts it in her mouth and practically rolls her eyes. 'These are seriously good. I think we might have to eat here every night this week.'

'No argument from me.'

Candy watches me skewer a mussel and wash it down with the rest of my wine.

'Is she with anyone at the moment?' she asks.

'Who, Mum?'

Candy nods.

'I have no idea. Probably. She's never really managed very well on her own, has she? Not that she needs a man, I think she likes to be wanted, that's her problem. Trouble is the blokes she goes for have always remained about the same age, somewhere in their thirties, despite the fact that she's gotten older. She's asking for trouble.'

'She might change one day.'

I snort. 'That I'd like to see – the day Mum grows up and stops messing about with toy boys.'

'Talking of which, have you seen those guys over on the table in the restaurant next to us? Don't look now.'

I resist turning around. 'What about them?'

'They're pretty hot – almost as good looking as that guy you fancied on the boat this morning.'

'I thought *you* were planning on having a man-free holiday?'

'Oh, that's a shame,' Candy says sweeping her caramel blonde hair behind her ears. 'Looks like their girlfriends have turned up.'

'Just as well, otherwise you'd have been straight over there.'

'Seriously, Sophie, you make me sound desperate and really I'm not, I promise,' she giggles into her wine.

I glance behind me. A curvy girl with straight black hair is being kissed on both cheeks by one of the men at the table. She sits down next to him and his hand rests on the small of her back. Their laughter and chatter is caught on the wind, then swallowed up by the rhythmic beat of the Greek music drifting towards us. I turn back to Candy and our table. Even though she goes about it in a reckless way, I get why Mum doesn't want to be alone – I miss the comfort and familiarity of a boyfriend, of always having someone there for you. Like a best friend. I shake the thought from my head and pour Candy and me some more wine.

Chapter Three

I'm glad Candy offered to drive to Myrtos beach. Not only do I get to look at the scenery whizz by as we drive inland from Fiskardo, past fir and cyprus tree clad hillsides, but I don't have to be the one to navigate winding Greek roads. The first part of the journey I recognise from our taxi drive to the hotel the first day we got here, but when we turn off and head towards Myrtos we're on new territory driving through villages with cream houses and red-tiled roofs, the surrounding countryside tree-lined with glimpses of limestone rocks between.

Our first sighting of endless blue sea leaves us speechless. We zigzag down the road cut into the limestone cliff, ignoring the graffiti scrawled on the low wall where the road has been dug into the hillside, and looking instead at the long swathe of sand below and the water sparkling in the sunshine.

We park up alongside dozens of other cars on the dusty parking area and heave our rucksacks out of the boot loaded with everything we need for the day: sunscreen, beach towels, a book each, bottled water and a packed lunch prepared for us by the hotel.

The beach looks exactly as it does in photos, except better. The sea is turquoise turning a deeper blue towards the horizon, the sand gleams and the tree-studded limestone cliffs tower above the crescent of sand. We walk the short distance from our car, past the small beach bar and on to the sand.

'We're nearly halfway through our holiday already.' I sigh

as we crunch in our flip-flops over the tiny pale grey pebbles that make up the beach.

'Glass half full, Sophie – we've got more than half our holiday still left.'

'Sorry, I don't mean to be negative, it's just I'm loving being here and I don't want it to end.'

'I totally agree with you there.'

Four rows of sunloungers line the centre of the beach in front of the beach bar. Although it's still early, there are plenty of people already camped out beneath the umbrellas with more sunbathers with their own lilos and umbrellas at the quieter ends of the beach. I spot two empty loungers sharing an umbrella at the end of the first row and lead the way to them.

'Perfect,' Candy says, with her hands on her hips. She gazes out at the uninterrupted view of sand and sea in front of us.

We lay our beach towels out on the sunloungers and settle down with our books. The waiter from the beach bar comes over and we order drinks.

I sip my lemonade and rest my head back, staring out across the sea shimmering in the heat. It's the perfect temperature: hot and dry, none of the rubbish humidity we're plagued with summer long back home. I can't work out where I'd reach by sailing straight ahead – maybe Italy. It doesn't look like there's anything out there, only endless ocean.

'Can you imagine living here and having beaches like this within driving distance?' Candy pushes her sunglasses into her hair and gazes out at the ocean.

'We do have the Gower Peninsula back home – it's a version of this, just as beautiful but in a different way.'

'True, but it's not *this*.' Candy gestures along the length of beach. 'You don't get drinks brought to you on the beaches in the Gower. And there isn't this weather.'

It is pretty special. I lean my head back on my sunlounger and close my eyes. Even beneath the shade of the umbrella I can feel the heat from the sun beating down, warming every inch of me. I want this moment to last forever; this feeling of contentment with no cares in the world to disturb my thoughts – apart from where we're going to go for dinner and what we should do tomorrow. The strained relationship with my mum and my discontentment with my job have faded away. I settle down to a few hours of sunbathing, swimming, reading and another drink or two.

It's late in the afternoon by the time we get back to our hotel. We shower and change into clean, sand-free clothes and decide to head into town for dinner followed by cocktails and an early night. We take a walk along the harbourside starting from the end furthest from our hotel, passing the café where we had frappés on Sunday and the stall where Candy bought her necklace. *Artemis* is moored in the same place and there's movement on board. I know before Candy even opens her mouth what she's going to do.

'Hello!' she shouts down to the man standing on the deck. He's red-faced and sweaty in a T-shirt smeared with oil and the short sleeves rolled right up showing off muscly shoulders. 'Do you speak English?'

The man spreads his hands and then points to his chest. 'Of course.'

'Good. Do you do day trips?'

Before he answers another man emerges from below deck. I take a sharp breath as I realise it's the man who caught my eye when Candy was bartering over her necklace. He steps on to the deck, his feet bare like they were when I first saw him but he has a T-shirt on this time. The man talking to us turns to his friend and rattles something off in Greek.

The other man nods back. '*Ne, fysika.*' He turns to Candy. 'You want to go for a boat ride?'

'We'd like to see some of the quieter beaches that aren't easy to get to, if possible. Don't we?' She turns to me.

The man's eyes flick to mine and I smile.

He steps up on to the edge of the boat and hops across to the solid ground of the harbourside.

'We can take you out on Wednesday?' he says, moving the silver cross around his neck between his thumb and finger.

'Great, that'll be perfect, thank you.'

'I'm Alekos,' he says, shaking Candy's hand then mine.

'Hello,' I say. He really is handsome up close: tall with deep hazel eyes, tanned skin and just the right amount of stubble.

'I'm Candy and this is Sophie.'

'My friend Demetrius,' Alekos says, motioning towards the boat. 'He's the skipper.'

I've lost the ability to speak. I feel a fool, unable to make small talk. Candy and Alekos are discussing payment for hiring the boat for the day. The way Alekos runs his hand through his hair sends shivers through me. I really have been single for too long.

Candy passes Alekos some euros and he shakes her hand again. Alekos turns to go and Candy says, 'Do you know anywhere good we can go out dancing tomorrow night?'

'Retro, plays live Greek music, just on the edge of town.'

'Is that where you both go?' she says with a nod towards Demetrius.

'Sometimes,' Alekos says and grins.

'Great.' Candy hooks her arm in mine. 'We'll see you on Wednesday.' She manoeuvres us away until we're heading along the harbourside back towards the fish restaurant. She leans into me, giggling. 'Unless of course we see them before.'

'You're impossible. How much did you just spend for them to sail us around all day?'

'Enough. But money well spent, I'd say.' Candy squeezes my arm tight. 'He left you lost for words. Pretty damn hot and his friend's easy on the eye too – the quiet and moody type.'

She was right about that. Up close he might have been a disappointment but he was quite the opposite. I guess that's the advantage of having a friend with the confidence to walk right up to strangers like that. I'd never have had the nerve to talk to him, not even about a boat trip, a genuine reason. Hopefully he just thought I was shy rather than a blushing crazy person.

Chapter Four

The summer before we went to university, Candy and I spent most Friday and Saturday nights clubbing at Odyssey in Bristol. It's only seven years ago but it feels like a lifetime. Occasionally we'd bump into my mum there and sometimes she'd come out with Candy and me and our friends. She was only in her mid-thirties then and acted and looked younger than that anyway. Those were the days when Mum was as good a friend as Candy. Candy loved to dance and I was okay once I'd had a few drinks. I always needed a bit of Dutch courage before wiggling my hips and not being totally grossed out by some horny lad grinding against me.

Tonight is different; we're in Greece where the vibe is more chilled than in the UK – I get the feeling people go out to socialise rather than on a mission to get drunk. Gone is the commotion of trying to get served at a packed bar, catching the eye of the barman, shouting your order above thumping music and the mass of other people shouting next to you. It's sophisticated in Greece, where a waiter or waitress takes your order at your table and returns with your drinks *and* complimentary nibbles: crisps, nuts and biscuits. What's not to like?

After dinner and drinks by the water, we manage to find our way through the maze of Fiskardo's back streets to the bar on the hillside Alekos had told us about the day before.

Candy hooks her arm in mine as we weave our way across a packed dance floor to the seating area on the other side.

Lamps throw warm light on to the aubergine-coloured walls packed with retro-style film prints; sofas and chairs tuck snugly into the corners and there's a raised stage along one wall where a live band plays catchy Greek music with a modern vibe.

'I'm glad we listened to him,' Candy shouts in my ear. We find two velvet-covered chairs next to a small table at the back of the bar. 'This place is great.'

'Local knowledge,' I reply. 'Always the best.'

'Doesn't necessarily mean someone's got taste though.'

'True, but he looked like someone who would have taste.'

Candy laughs. 'But of course, you would think that. You seriously like him.'

I shrug. 'I don't know him to know if I *like* him – he caught my eye that's all.'

A waitress stops by our table with an empty tray in her hand and a smile on her face. '*Yasas*,' she says with a nod. '*Ti tha thelate?*'

'Um, two glasses of wine, err *krasi*, please,' I say.

'Of course,' she replies in perfect English. 'Red or white?'

'Red please.'

Despite how busy it is, the waitress is back in no time with our wine and a selection of savoury nibbles in two bowls. She places them on the small table between us along with the bill tucked into a shot glass.

'This is the life.' Candy clinks her glass of wine against mine. 'I don't want this week to end.'

'At least you've got an exciting job to go back to when we go home. I've got the same old boring 9 to 5.'

'At least it's related to your degree.'

I take a sip of the wine, slightly sweet and delicious. 'But it's not what I want to be doing as a career, long term at least.'

'Make a change then. Use this week to kick start how you want the rest of your life to pan out. Find a new job. Or go freelance.' Candy looks at me over the top of her wine glass. 'You know you want to.'

'It just seems so reckless when I have a perfectly good job, working with nice people, earning decent money.'

'Ack,' she says, sticking her tongue out and wrinkling her nose. 'Sometimes you've just gotta take a chance. So, take a chance. That's what I did to get my job on *Casualty* and you know how well that's worked out for me.' She grabs my arm and leans towards me. 'Look who's just walked in.'

My eyes follow the direction Candy's looking and my heart skips a beat. Alekos, along with Demetrius, is on the far side of the dance floor, dressed simply in jeans and a white T-shirt, talking to a group of men by the bar. One of the men grips Alekos' shoulder and they laugh together. It's silly how weak at the knees he makes me feel, like a movie star has just walked in – Johnny Depp or Leonardo DiCaprio. I guess film star looks, those deep hazel eyes and a body as good as his can have that effect.

'Do you think they were coming here tonight anyway when they suggested this place,' Candy says. 'Or do you think they've turned up hoping we'd be here?'

'Candy, stop reading into it – he said they come here sometimes. I doubt very much they've come in the hope of seeing us. Anyway, we don't even know if they have girlfriends.' I take a handful of crisps from the bowl on our table. 'They probably do have girlfriends and even if they don't I'm sure they have the pick of all the girls on this island.'

'Or, like I said, they came in the hope of seeing us again,' Candy says with a smile over the top of her glass. She takes a sip. 'You have so little faith in just how attractive you are.'

I wave my hand at her and shake my head.

'See, my point exactly,' Candy says. 'You've got to learn how to take a compliment. If there's one thing you should have learnt from your mum it's confidence and how to smile sweetly when someone says something nice about you.'

I lean forward and raise my voice as the band starts up again with an energetic tune. 'Yeah but you could argue my mum has far too much confidence. She'd be able to come into this bar and ten minutes later leave with a bloke – a good looking one too. That's not something I aspire to.'

'Me neither,' Candy says and smirks when I shoot her a look. 'But a little more confidence and faith in yourself wouldn't go amiss now would it?'

'I guess not.' I lean back in my chair and take a sip of my wine. A fan whirrs above me hard at work to combat the heat. I glance across to the bar but Alekos has been swallowed up by all the people that flooded the dance floor when the up-tempo song started playing. I'm surprised Candy hasn't dragged me out there yet.

'Do you think your mum will ever settle down?'

I shrug. 'Who knows? She's got to stop choosing unsuitable men first. I mean they're either loads younger than her and don't want the commitment or are flipping married and just happy to have a mindless affair. Why she chooses men like that I have no idea. It's like she wants to have a complicated relationship that makes it easy to end when she's had enough of them.'

'Or it's simply because she's commitment-phobic and choosing men like that ensures they're never going to be like "oh marry me, Leila".'

'You're probably right.'

Candy looks at me wide-eyed and starts flapping her hand rapidly at me.

I frown and then a firm hand grasps my shoulder.

Alekos pulls up a stool and sits down next to me with a bottle of beer in his hand. 'You like my suggestion then.'

'Candy likes to dance,' I say, glancing between him and Demetrius, who's pulled up a chair next to Candy.

'Sophie does too, although most times she has to be dragged on to a dance floor.'

Alekos' jean-clad knee is touching mine. I wonder if it's intentional or if it's purely because there's not much space around our table.

'You like to dance?' Demetrius turns to Candy and holds out his hand.

'I do indeed,' Candy replies with a grin. She gives me a sly glance as she takes Demetrius' hand and he pulls her towards the dance floor.

'I love the music,' I say, watching Candy and Demetrius wind their way between people. 'It's different to what I imagined when you said it was live music. It sounds more contemporary than I thought it would be.'

'The music always very good here. I play here before,' Alekos says, gesturing towards the live band.

'What, the guitar?'

He nods and leans closer to me so I can hear him above the music, stamping feet and chatter. 'I love it. I write too.'

'Music or stories?'

'Music, but it tells a story too.' He's so close his breath tickles the side of my face and sends shivers through me.

'Are you in a band?'

'Sort of,' he says, watching the musicians as they launch into an even more upbeat song than the previous one. 'I got to know a few musicians and a singer the first summer I was here. She liked my guitar playing so hired me for gigs.'

I can only imagine how captivating he must be sat playing a guitar. 'So you're a musician and a co-skipper on a boat.'

'For a couple of summers, yes.' He takes a sip of his beer and places it on the table next to my wine. 'What do you do back in England?'

'Nothing as exciting or as interesting as you.'

'Tell me.'

'I work for a large advertising company doing graphic design for banks and shops.'

'It sound good.'

I nod. 'It is a good job – it's decent pay and I work with great people but it's not what I want to be doing. It's not what I intended doing when I graduated from my illustration degree.'

'What would you like to do?'

'Something more creative and less commercial.'

I can hardly hear him above the beat of the music. I shuffle in my seat so I'm facing him. I've lost sight of Candy and Demetrius in the crush on the dance floor.

'I know how you feel. I work on Cephalonia only for the summer – the rest of the time I work at my parents' restaurant on the mainland.'

'And it's not what you want to do either?'

'I love it but it very different to life here.'

I pick up my wine glass and tap it against his beer. 'To us both one day achieving our dreams.'

He taps my glass back. 'I drink to that.'

We down the remainder of our drinks and laugh as we knock into each other putting our empty glasses back on the table.

'When you told us about this place did you know you were going to be here this evening too?' I ask, remembering back to Candy's comment when Alekos and Demetrius had walked in.

He touches his chest and looks at me with mock helplessness. 'You say I plan this?'

I laugh. 'I think Candy was hoping we'd bump into you again, that's why she asked.'

In the dim light I catch sight of Candy dancing with Demetrius, their arms encircling each other, their hips moving together. The feel of Alekos' thigh against mine is too much – I've never wanted someone to kiss me as badly as I do right now.

'She wanted to see Demetrius again?' Alekos says close to my ear.

I turn to face him and take a deep breath. 'No, it was because I wanted to see you again.' Our faces are inches away from each other.

I'm not sure if I move closer or he does, but the next thing I know his lips are on mine, his strong arms pulling me close. I kiss him back and it feels as if the bar, the music, all the people, Candy and Demetrius included, peel away from around us, until it's just Alekos and me locked together in an embrace. His stubble grazes my cheeks, our tongues find each other and his hands reach for my face and caress my skin.

'Is this what you were hoping for?'

I laugh and my cheeks flush hot. 'Something like that. Let's just say you caught my eye.'

He leans closer, his hands sliding along my bare legs, stopping just beneath my short skirt. I kiss him again, aware of the voices and the music around me, his firm touch, the taste of beer on his lips.

'You two should really get a room.' Candy's hand lands on my shoulder and the moment with Alekos is lost. We pull away from each other and I catch Demetrius wink at Alekos as he slaps him on his back.

This is what I wanted from the moment I first caught sight of him on *Artemis*, although I guess I envisaged something more romantic than a drunken kiss in a bar. I'm heady with alcohol, hot from the stuffy confines of the dark and atmospheric bar. Alekos' hand finds mine and I meet his smiling eyes.

'So tomorrow,' Candy says, shooting me a grin. 'You still okay to take us sailing at ten? You won't be too hungover?'

'I'll be fine, Demetrius maybe not.' Alekos flicks Demetrius' stomach with his fingers.

'It no problem.' Demetrius puts his arm around Candy. 'You should bring bag for overnight – we can take you to one of the best beaches on Cephalonia but we need two days.'

Alekos' hand tightens just a fraction in mine and Candy catches my eye. I know we're all thinking the same thing – spending the night on the boat has the potential to lead to a lot more than what's happened tonight.

'It sounds amazing,' I say. 'But, I, um…'

'Oh, what the hell, Sophie, we're on holiday.'

I take a deep breath. 'Okay, it really does sound amazing.' Alekos' hand relaxes again.

'There's a beach on the north-west coast that can only be reached by boat – the best,' Alekos says.

'This early in the summer will be very quiet.' Demetrius pulls Candy closer to him. '*Pame exo.*' He gestures towards the entrance and Candy nods and follows him back across the crowded dance floor.

I stand up and smooth down my skirt. Alekos tucks a ten euro note in the shot glass on the table and together we follow after Candy and Demetrius. He catches my hand in the dimly lit corridor between the bar and the entrance.

'We see you tomorrow.' His thumb rhythmically rubs up and down mine. I don't want his touch to end and I'm longing to feel his hands all over me. Demetrius and Candy are already outside, Candy with her back to the bar wall, Demetrius' hands on her breasts as they kiss. Alekos notices too. He leans down and lightly kisses my lips. 'Tomorrow,' he says, letting go of my hand. He saunters outside and grabs the collar of Demetrius' shirt.

'*Ela*.' He pulls Demetrius away from Candy. '*Kalinikta*,' he calls back with a wave.

It's a fresh night out and the shock of cool air after the heat of the bar makes me shiver. The walk back to our hotel sobers me up. It's good to get back to our room and kick off my pumps.

'So much for a man-free holiday,' Candy says, as we flop on to our beds.

'You started this. You stopped and asked them about the boat trip.'

'Sophie, my lovely, I think you started this by fancying the pants off Alekos to begin with.'

'You like Demetrius?'

'Well, we've hardly said two words to each other but it helps that he's seriously fit.'

I throw a pillow at her and we fall about giggling.

Chapter Five

I wake at the sound of a door closing. With my heart thudding, my eyes fly open and I scramble to sit up. Candy is already dressed and holding a plastic bag in her hand.

I rub my eyes and frown at the pulsing feeling across my forehead. 'What time is it?'

'Nearly nine.'

'Where on earth have you been?'

She tips the contents of the bag on to the end of my bed. Spread out on the sheet are a couple of bottles of water, chewing gum, and condoms. Lots of condoms.

'I thought we should go prepared.'

'You are kidding me?'

Candy sits on the end of my bed. 'What, you want to end up on a boat, miles from anywhere, dying to shag Alekos and have no contraception with you?'

I rub my temples, too dehydrated and hungover to be thinking about having sex with a man I barely know.

'I'm being sensible and responsible,' she says and puts her hands on her hips.

'I didn't say yes to staying on the boat overnight just because I want to have sex with Alekos,' I say.

'Ha ha! But you *do* want to.'

'You're impossible.' I smile.

'Well, just in case you decide to unleash your naughty side tonight, have these.' A pack of condoms flies across the bed and lands in my lap.

~

I have butterflies in my stomach as we walk through the hotel grounds and past the inviting pool. It's not quite ten in the morning and the sun wraps itself around me. It's another perfect day with not a cloud to be seen. The blue sea and sky merge together as one. I'm not sure if the fluttering feeling in my stomach is a good or bad thing – am I nervous about putting myself in this position with Alekos, or is it the excitement and anticipation of what may happen in the next twenty-four hours? My rucksack is slung over my shoulder with a change of clothes, my wash bag, sunscreen, a bottle of water and the condoms. The fluttering in my chest intensifies.

'You're very quiet,' Candy says, as the view towards the harbour opens up before us.

I catch sight of *Artemis* and stop. 'Are you sure we should be doing this?'

Candy stops a couple of paces in front of me and turns round. 'You think about things too much. Stop worrying.'

She starts walking again and I catch her arm.

'I mean we don't really know them, is it actually a good idea to be spending a night on the boat who knows where?'

'We were going sailing with them today anyway, what difference does it make if we stay a bit longer?'

'You know exactly what I'm talking about.'

Candy puts her arm round my shoulders. 'See what you feel like when you see him again and if you still feel funny about it, then we do what we've paid them for – a day trip.'

I bite my lip, take a deep breath and start walking again. I've been single for too long and always too choosy about boyfriends. Having a mother who had so many one-night stands and short term boyfriends over the years made me go the other way and now this – a night aboard *Artemis* with Alekos and Demetrius feels exactly like something Mum would do.

They're waiting for us, both relaxing on deck smoking a cigarette. Alekos catches sight of us, grinds out his cigarette in an ashtray and waves. I wave back, the fluttering feeling turning into longing, for him to kiss me again and put his arms around me. I catch hold of Candy's hand and squeeze it.

'You were right,' I say under my breath as we reach the boat. 'I was worrying about nothing.'

'*Kalimera*,' Alekos says, holding out his hand. I take hold of it, warm and firm in mine, and hop across from the harbourside and on to the boat.

'*Kalimera*,' I say to Demetrius.

He nods and stubs out his cigarette. '*Kalimera*.'

He seems to be a man of few words and I haven't worked out if he's just shy, a little rude or maybe after last night, hungover. I hope Candy doesn't end up regretting this.

We sail out of the harbour. Fiskardo gets further and further away, its bubblegum pink, saffron yellow and sky blue buildings getting smaller as they blur into a candyfloss line of colour. The sun beats down and I'm glad of my new sunhat and the slight breeze wrapping around us as we cut through the gentle movement of the sea. I relax back next to Candy on the deck and take a sip from a cold bottle of beer. Refreshing and crisp, it's even better on a boat on the Ionian Sea under a hot sun than on a summer's day in a pub garden back home. It doesn't take long for Alekos to remove his T-shirt and he's how I first saw him, all tanned skin and taut muscles and as delicious as I remember. Life can't get much better than this.

We keep Cephalonia in sight as we sail south. With Demetrius and Alekos working together as a perfect team, there's nothing for Candy and me to do apart from soak up the sun on the deck. My tan is non-existent compared to Candy's, but with sunscreen slathered on I relish the warmth of the sun on my body beneath my beach kaftan.

Alekos and Demetrius keep busy, Alekos disappearing occasionally below deck to the tiny galley kitchen, Demetrius sailing the boat, while Candy and I sunbathe and read and watch the Cephalonian coastline pass by.

After sailing for a couple of hours we round a headland and a stretch of beach dotted with umbrellas with a rocky outcrop of rocks jutting into the sea is revealed. The sea changes from deepest blue to a perfect turquoise and when I look over the side of the boat I can clearly see down to the sandy floor.

'We stop for swim, fishing and lunch,' Demetrius says, dropping the anchor over the side. He peels off his T-shirt and dives into the water.

Alekos appears back on deck with a tray of food and places it between Candy and me. 'While Demetrius sails, I make lunch.'

'Wow,' we both say in unison.

My mouth waters at the sight of a large bowl of Greek salad, a crusty loaf of white bread, skewered chicken and bottles of Coke.

'Is this what you do at your parents' restaurant back home?' I ask, as Alekos passes me a bottle and a skewer of chicken.

'*Ochi.*' He shakes his head. 'Mama would laugh. Doesn't trust me in her kitchen. I work in the restaurant, in charge of the waiters.'

'Well, this is seriously delicious,' Candy says, with a mouthful of Greek salad.

Demetrius reappears over the other side of the boat and pulls himself up, dripping seawater on to the deck. He grabs a towel and rubs it through his hair before drying his chest, sitting down next to Alekos and taking a chunk of bread.

'Enjoy your swim?' Candy tugs a piece of chicken off one of the skewers.

'The water perfect here,' Demetrius replies, catching Candy's eye. 'You should swim after.'

'I'm not sure I'm going to be able to move after I've eaten this.'

'You help me fish for dinner instead.'

We eat everything and while Alekos clears away, Candy heads down to the end of the boat with Demetrius. He sets up a fishing rod and curls his free arm around Candy as she sits snugly in front of him.

I lie down on the cushions on the deck and close my eyes, feeling comfortably full and wanting my food to digest before diving into the water to cool off. The boat rocks slightly with the movement of the sea and I must have dozed off because the next thing I know fingers are tickling my sides. My eyes fly open. Alekos is leaning over me wearing only a pair of swimming trunks.

'You want to have a swim?'

He holds his hand out. I take it and he pulls me to my feet. I slip my kaftan off revealing my blue bikini. I follow Alekos down the ladder on the side of the boat. The water shocks my skin and makes it tingle, but it only takes a few seconds for my body to adjust to the cooler temperature.

I swim after Alekos and away from *Artemis* until I'm floating in the cool, clear water between the beach dotted with a handful of sunbathers and the boat. I push my legs down and realise my toes touch the sandy bottom. I launch myself up off the ocean floor until I'm on my back, keeping afloat by gently kicking my feet and running my hands through the water, gazing up at the blue sky peppered with wispy clouds.

Alekos swims towards me, his tanned shoulders clenching each time he pushes his arms through the water. He circles me and flips over on to his back, joining me staring up at the sky.

'One of the best places to swim and fish,' he says.

'It's magical.'

It truly is – a place where you can forget about everything back home. It's like we're living an alternate life here; I guess in a way we really are – a few days of make believe before the reality of having to return home kicks in. I shove the thought to the back of my mind and make a pact with myself to live in the moment.

Alekos swims further out and I stay towards the shallows, happy to bob up and down on the gentle swell of the sea.

There's a screech from *Artemis* and I splash around in time to see Candy, with Demetrius' help, reel in a fish on to the boat.

'Our dinner!' she calls across to me with a grin. 'Come on, you two; Demetrius wants to get going again!'

Alekos starts swimming back towards the boat and I set off too, speeding through the clear water. I reach the boat just before Alekos does and pull myself up on to the ladder.

'We're not staying here for the rest of the day then?' I ask as I climb back on board. Alekos gives me a cheeky nudge as I reach the top. I grab a towel and flick it at him. He catches me and pulls me towards him until there's just the towel between us and his strong arms wrapped around my waist.

'Now we take you to the best beach on Cephalonia.'

Chapter Six

The deserted beach is hugged on three sides by pale grey cliffs, almost as towering as the ones overlooking Myrtos beach and equally as impressive. The water is deep enough for Demetrius to drop anchor quite close to the shore. There's no other way to get to the beach apart from by boat and I love that it's an empty stretch of sand. I thought the last beach we stopped at was stunning, but this one blows my mind.

Alekos jumps down off the side of the boat first and the water reaches his waist. He offers his hand and I take it, splashing down next to him, relishing the pleasant shock of cold seawater that hasn't yet had the summer sun to heat it.

Alekos helps Candy down and her shriek as she hits the water swiftly turns to giggles.

'Go to the beach and we'll bring stuff across,' Alekos says.

I hook my arm in Candy's and we wade through the shallows together, our feet sinking into the sand with every step we take. It's late afternoon and I have that contented sleepy feeling from too much sun and a couple of beers.

'You're getting on very well with Demetrius.' We reach the beach and turn back to see Demetrius passing lilos and umbrellas down to Alekos.

'I can say the same for you and Alekos.'

I squeeze her arm tighter. 'You two earlier was like watching that scene from *Ghost* except with a fishing rod instead of a potter's wheel.'

Candy laughs. 'Seriously, I never realised fishing could be

so sexy. At least it is on a Greek island, with a hot Greek, on a boat floating on the Ionian Sea with the sun beating down.'

Alekos and Demetrius join us on the beach, arms loaded with everything we need for the next few hours – lilos to relax on, beach towels, kindling and wood to make a fire and a large cool box containing the fish packed in ice.

Our feet sink into the sand as we walk to the middle of the beach and the water that rhythmically laps the sand is so clear and turquoise that if it was in a travel brochure I'd think it had been photo-shopped. It's almost a shame to taint the perfect expanse of sand by leaving our footprints snaking across it. Almost a shame. The other half of me relishes us being the only people here.

The sun is setting by the time we get the fire going and have a final splash about in the sea. Demetrius wraps the fish he and Candy caught earlier in tin foil, and tucks the shiny silver packages in the embers of the fire.

'Photo time!' Candy says, pulling her camera from out of her bag.

'Wait,' Alekos says. He reaches into the ice box and takes out an octopus. 'Caught fresh this morning from a man I know in Fiskardo.'

He holds it in one hand while his other hand shades his eyes from the sun. His hair is short and damp and his chest is still beaded with seawater. Candy takes a photo and then Demetrius joins Alekos. Candy turns the camera on me and I smile, feeling happier than I have in a very long time.

I rest back on my hand and take a sip of beer from a bottle and watch Alekos tuck the octopus into a foil package with lemon halves and push it into the fire. A blaze of pink, amber and a fiery red seeps across the darkening sky, bleeding into the calm ocean. This is perfection. Candy catches my eye and grins. In the firelight her tan looks deeper than it really is. Even my skin looks like I've spent the summer in the sun rather than just a few days.

Alekos and Demetrius drag the foil packages out of the fire with sticks and somehow, without burning their fingers, they manage to open them up, releasing the steam into the dusky air. My mouth waters as Demetrius liberally squeezes lemon over the fish.

'Let's eat.' Alekos places the octopus in its foil on top of a chopping board and slices it into bite-sized chunks. Demetrius puts one of the fish parcels in front of Candy and squeezes more lemon over it.

I sit across from them next to Alekos. In the dusky light, the fire throws warmth and flickering shadows across our faces. Alekos passes the octopus to Demetrius and he hands it to Candy. She takes a piece and pops it in her mouth.

'I've never tasted anything so good.'

'It fresh. The best,' Demetrius says, passing the package to me.

I take a bite and relish the citrus tang and the perfect firmness of the octopus.

I smile at Alekos. 'You can't get much better than this.' Sand spreads out in both directions, the sea laps at the shore and the sun melts into the horizon. *Artemis* bobs on the slightest movement of the sea, lit by lamps so we can wade through the water and find our way back in the dark. The thought that this is our own slice of paradise is the icing on the cake.

Alekos flakes a piece of fish from the foil parcel on the sand in front of him and hands it to me.

I close my eyes and chew. 'Oh my God that is good.'

'Does this beach have a name?' Candy asks, taking a sip from the bottle of beer Demetrius passes to her.

'Platia Ammos,' Alekos says.

'My sister would love this place.' Candy wipes her hands on one of the beach towels.

'Although Phoebe has seen her fair share of beautiful places,' I say.

'She went travelling for a year before going to university,' Candy explains. 'Spent six months in Australia and learnt to surf and scuba-dive. She's a total beach bum and loves desolate beaches. The quieter the better.'

Alekos turns to me. 'Do you have brother or sister?'

I shake my head. 'No, just me.' I lean forward and pull at the white flesh of the baked fish in front of me, flaking it off the skin.

'What about your parents? Where are they?'

Candy catches my eye from across the other side of the fire.

'My mum doesn't live far from me in Bristol but we don't really talk any longer. And I don't know my dad.'

'You don't know him? At all?' Alekos' hand brushes mine as we both reach for more fish.

'It's complicated,' I say, not willing to share any more with him despite feeling like he's someone I could reveal everything to. I don't want to scare him away with my messed up family.

'I have typical big Greek family,' Alekos says to fill the silence. I'm not sure if he's understood my hint that I don't want to talk about my family or that he's simply happy to talk about his. Either way I'm glad the attention is back on him.

'I have an older sister married with a little son, Yannis, and my parents who run our restaurant. Plus grandparents and many aunts and uncles.'

'This is on the mainland though, where you come from?'

He nods. 'It very different to island life but we live between the sea and the mountain. It still very beautiful.'

'It sounds it.' I wipe my hands on a napkin and rest back on my elbows in the sand. 'You can see the sea from where you live?'

'No, but we can see Mount Olympus.'

'Wow,' Candy says. 'That's your view? I thought I was lucky having a view over our local park from my house.'

The view from my bedroom window is over the courtyard garden of the off-licence below our flat. I open the curtains to the sight of bins, concrete paving and a couple of pots with dead flowers in. It's a different world here; a different lifestyle completely.

Demetrius stands up, reaches his hand out and pulls Candy to her feet. 'Come with me.'

Still holding his hand, Candy downs the rest of her beer,

turns to us and with a wink at me says, 'See you guys later.'

'See you later,' I say.

Alekos and I watch them walk hand in hand along the beach. It'll be dark soon, the only light the glow of the fire, the lights on *Artemis* and the stars above.

Alekos reaches for more fish. 'Don't let it go to waste,' he says, breaking the silence.

I sit back up and pop another handful of the lemony fish into my mouth. 'How long have you been working on Cephalonia?'

'I spent the last two summers here with Demetrius.'

'I'm so jealous that you get to spend the rest of this summer here too.'

He shakes his head. 'Not this time, only the early part of the season.'

'Why?'

'*Yiati*… Because Mama needs me back to work at the restaurant this summer.'

'Oh no, that's a shame.'

He shrugs. 'It is life.'

But what a life it must be – not the worst thing in the world to be swapping summer on a boat sailing tourists around the Ionian Islands for living and working in a place where the backdrop is the mountain of the gods. 'Well, your life on the mainland beats my life, my job and my view back in the UK.'

'I like my job,' Alekos says. 'I like that it is a family business.'

'Will you miss all this though?' I wave my hand in front of us, the dusky light casting a pink glow over the sand and the gentle waves curling on to the shore.

'Of course I will miss this. And you.'

It takes me a moment to digest what he's said – I hope he can't see me blushing in this half-light. There's just something about him that turns me to jelly and I can barely keep control of my emotions.

'I'm going to miss you too.'

Alekos reaches across the short distance between us and

takes my hand in his. 'I wish we met earlier. That we have more time together.'

Candy and Demetrius are further along the shore, splashing about in the shallows, still holding hands and giggling together.

I glance at Alekos, my cheeks burning from the thoughts tumbling around my head of just how much I want him.

'It's thanks to Candy that we did meet – I'd never have had the nerve to talk to you without her.'

'Then thank you, Candy!' He grins and strokes his thumb along mine. 'You don't have a boyfriend back home?'

I laugh and shake my head. 'No, there's no one back home.'

'*Kala*. Good,' he says.

'What about you? No girlfriend waiting for you back on the mainland?'

'No one, I promise. There no time for a girlfriend. I'm always working or too busy with volleyball or writing music. Mama wants me to have a girlfriend. My older sister is married and has a baby, so Mama thinks my turn next.'

'At least I've never had that pressure from my mum. Although she's always with someone, she's never been married herself so isn't bothered one way or another if I end up marrying or not.'

'Our mothers very different.'

'It's probably just a cultural thing.'

Candy and Demetrius are standing in the shallows, kissing. It's not dark enough to ignore Demetrius' hands beneath Candy's kaftan, firmly planted on her bum.

Alekos glances over and turns back to me. 'They like each other.'

'They certainly do.'

With their arms slung around each other's waists they wade through the water and climb up on to *Artemis*.

With the light fading rapidly, the crescent of beach is empty apart from me and Alekos.

Chapter Seven

Alekos looks at me, like really looks at me. Even in the semi-darkness I can feel his hazel eyes boring into me as his hand reaches for my cheek. Candy and Demetrius are back on the boat, drunk and getting up to no good no doubt, Paul back home forgotten. I have no one back home, so why do I feel hesitant about what I know is going to happen next? I'm tipsy but not drunk like Candy and I fancy Alekos… God do I fancy him. Candy would tell me off for thinking things through too much, that I should be living in the moment

Alekos kisses me. Any doubts disappear the moment I kiss him back. He's delicious – an intoxicating combination of stubble grazing my cheeks, the scent of the ocean and aftershave and salt and lemon on his skin and lips.

He gently pushes me down alongside the smouldering embers of the fire until I'm lying in the sand, cushioned by the warm grains with only the stars and sliver of moon throwing any light on us.

'You're beautiful, Sophie.' He caresses the side of my face and runs his hands down the length of my body until he reaches my thighs. I bite my lip as his lips brush against my stomach and he wiggles my kaftan up and over my head, leaving it crumpled in the sand next to us. I lie back down, the tiny grains of sand digging into my back offset by Alekos' gentle kisses moving up my stomach and over my breasts to my neck. The sky above is darkening, the only sound the hush of the waves lapping the shore, our breathing and the occasional crackle from the fire.

Alekos kisses me again, his toned chest pressing against mine. 'We can go back to the boat if you want?'

I don't want this to stop – I don't want to be sensible and indoors or interrupt the feeling that's coursing through me. I reach for my beach bag and take a condom out. Without a word I give him my answer by handing it to him and tugging down his shorts. He slides his hand beneath my bikini bottoms and pulls them off. I wrap my legs around him and close my eyes when he's finally inside me, moving silently and rhythmically against me.

'We were both pretty drunk last night,' Candy says after emerging from Demetrius' cabin the next morning. She sits next to me on the deck and rests her arm behind me.

I gaze out across the endless sparkling ocean to the horizon.

'You did it?'

She looks at me and rolls her eyes. 'Uh uh. Did you?' She grasps my arm. '*Did* you?'

I nod.

'Oh my God, Sophie Keech. I thought you two were going to just talk all night and that'd be it. You do realise I went off with Demetrius to give you a chance to shag Alekos.'

'Don't blame me for you doing the dirty with Demetrius. I know you, you don't do anything you don't want to do.'

Candy shrugs. 'I know, Demetrius is hot, I couldn't resist. But how was Alekos?'

I glance across to the remains of the fire on the beach, charred wood, black against pale sand and I imagine the imprint our bodies left. I don't want to talk about him like this – like he's some meaningless one-night stand, exactly what Demetrius is for Candy. Alekos is more than that. I swallow back tears, unnerved at how emotional I feel.

'Last night was the best of my life,' I say and mean it. 'I'm not just talking about the sex, although my God, it was so good – it was everything…'

My words trail off as Alekos emerges from below deck,

sunglasses wedged in his dark hair, a white T-shirt and pale blue shorts showing off his tan.

'Morning, Alekos,' Candy says and grins. 'I hear you had a good night last night.'

Alekos looks at me and I blush, but he smiles and winks at Candy. 'I heard you did too.'

It's Candy's turn to blush, exactly at the moment Demetrius steps on to the deck, his chest bare, sunglasses shading his eyes and an unlit cigarette between his lips.

'*Kalimera*,' he grunts, and paces to the furthest end of the boat. He sits and dangles his legs over the side.

Alekos points towards Demetrius. 'He not happy in the morning.' He looks at Candy and shrugs. 'Is normal.'

Candy sweeps her hair from her eyes. 'Whatever.'

Alekos steps towards me, leans in and kisses my forehead. '*Kalimera*.'

'*Kalimera*.' My heart somersaults around my chest.

'We get ready to sail. Leave in an hour.' He smiles and saunters down the boat and starts talking to Demetrius in Greek.

Candy grips my arm. 'He *really* likes you.'

'I'm sure Demetrius likes you too, he's just not a morning person.'

Candy leans towards me. 'Come on, me and Demetrius only happened because you and Alekos fancy each other. We were horny, that was all, a one-night stand that he's probably regretting because he has someone back home.'

'Like you do.'

'Exactly.' Candy leans back on her hands and stretches her long tanned legs out. 'It's a pretty sweet life this, spending the summer sailing around the islands, earning shitloads of money, picking up girls whenever they want and forgetting about life back home on the mainland.'

Is that all I am to Alekos? Another girl he's bedded over the summer; an easy English chick, impressed by the romance of a sailing boat and a secluded beach on a beautiful island. He's got the looks, the body… I wonder how many other girls he's seduced… But it felt like so much more – that kiss this morning, so tender, no sense of regret or embarrassment, unlike Demetrius.

Candy heads back below deck to bed with a hangover. It had been really late by the time Alekos and I had left the beach and gone back to the boat and down to his cabin. We heard Candy and Demetrius as we passed their cabin and it had been nearly dawn by the time we'd finally gone to sleep, curled in each other's arms. I'd woken before Alekos, with grains of sand on the sheet and in my hair. I'd showered, dressed and was the first one on deck until Candy had appeared.

While Candy sleeps and Alekos and Demetrius prepare the boat, I take a walk along the beach, past last night's remains of our bonfire. I shiver at the memory: the most perfect evening, roasting fish and an octopus over flames, talking to Alekos and finding out about his life, his English stilted at times but understandable with his deep voice and Greek accent and then… his touch, his taste, the feel of him…

I never want to forget my night with Alekos; I hadn't wanted it to end, for dawn to arrive and the magic to be broken. I sit down at the northern end of the beach and lean back on my hands, the limestone cliff soaring behind me. There's nothing apart from sand and ocean and *Artemis* floating on it. The rocks are craggy at the southern end of the beach, a handful of them jutting out into the sea.

Live for the moment. That's what Candy would say and indeed my mum, not that I'd want her opinion.

I stretch my toes and dig them into the sand, enjoying the feel of the cooler grains below the hot surface. Tomorrow we'll be on a plane heading home. Not that my life back home is bad – a good if predictable job, great colleagues, my housemates are fun. So okay, the state of our flat annoys me at times and after eighteen months of being single I quite fancy being in a relationship again, but life is good. I have money, lots of friends – surely that should make up for being single and having a non-existent relationship with my mum?

I'm being silly, this feeling isn't love, I've only known him for three days. It's the romance combined with falling in love with Cephalonia as much as anything – why would I want to return to my single life and my 9 to 5 job beneath humid grey skies in the UK when I could eat the freshest fish by the ocean, drink cocktails until dawn and make love to Alekos by moonlight on a deserted beach. I'm confusing lust for love.

'*Pame*!' Demetrius calls across to me from the boat. 'We go!'

I force the confusing feeling building in my chest to the back of my mind, scramble to my feet and walk back across the beach, leaving behind our multitude of crisscrossed footprints, the charred embers of the fire and the knowledge of where my body had been pressed into the sand with Alekos. I wade through the shallows and climb aboard *Artemis* and sit on the same spot on the deck where Candy and I had sat only the day before, when we first set sail from Fiskardo. It feels like a lifetime ago now, so much has happened, so much has changed in such a short time. Confusing emotions invade my thoughts again. I try to shake them off and empty my mind. I concentrate on watching the beach getting smaller and hazier as we sail away until it's out of sight completely.

Chapter Eight

Candy re-emerges from below deck by late morning. I'd underestimated just how much she'd drunk the night before. She's as hung over as Demetrius is moody. Regret is evident in his body language, in the way he reacts to Candy and how he pointedly chooses not to sit near her.

Alekos manages to make us feel as much at ease as he did the day before. We hug the coastline of Cephalonia, our senses bombarded by the taste of sea spray, the smell of sunscreen, the sight of beaches and cliffs and hidden coves revealed through lush greenery.

With Demetrius skippering *Artemis* and Alekos below deck preparing lunch I put my book down and turn to Candy. 'Are you okay?' I whisper.

She shoves her sunglasses into her hair and squints at me. 'Why wouldn't I be?'

'Um, you and Demetrius – you were all over each other last night and today, nothing. You fine with that?'

'It was a one-night stand – I always knew it was going to be. I don't regret it but if he does, that's his problem.'

'As long as you're okay.'

'Sophie, you know I am.' She pulls her sunglasses down over her eyes and rests her head back on a cushion.

We cut through the sea with ease only stopping to moor at Pessada, a fishing village on the southern coast. We eat lunch on *Artemis* and then Candy and I stroll along the coastal path to the village's tiny but stunning beach. The clear shallow water has rocks like submerged stepping stones scattered across the bay. Then we're off again heading around the foot of Cephalonia and up to Fiskardo. The closer we get, the more I long for our journey to never end. What will happen when we get back to the harbour? Will the magic of the last twenty-four hours disintegrate?

Fiskardo's in sight by the time Candy looks up from her book. She pushes her sunglasses down to the end of her nose and gazes towards the pastel-coloured outline of Fiskardo's seafront, then back at me. 'What do you want to do this evening?'

'Go to that fish restaurant, have a drink. What we've been doing all week.'

'So our usual night out in Fiskardo.' Candy laughs.

Demetrius steers *Artemis* while Alekos takes a break, sitting at the back of the boat drinking a bottle of Coke. I'm longing to join him, to sit next to him and chat – about our lives, our childhood, our jobs, our hopes, our dreams.

Candy leans closer and whispers. 'You should see him again tonight. Ask him out.'

'You want to spend our last evening with Demetrius?'

'Don't worry about me.'

I put my arm around Candy's shoulder. 'You're a good friend, you know.'

Candy laughs. 'I know.' She hooks her arm around my waist. 'We've had a good week, haven't we?'

'The best.' I mean it, for lots of reasons, not just for meeting Alekos. Spending time with Candy has been long overdue. 'We should do this again, make it a yearly thing.'

Candy nods. 'At least until we both get married and have kids.'

'Well, that's going to be so far in the future, I think we'll have plenty of holidays together before then.'

We sail into Fiskardo harbour and I'm amazed at how familiar the place feels. The waterfront is bustling with tourists and Greeks and the harbour itself is filled with gleaming white sailing boats. Demetrius steers us into the spot we left from and Candy and I sit and watch as Alekos, with a thick coiled rope in his hand, hops across from the boat to the jetty and helps pull the boat tight to the side of the dock and ties the rope securely.

'Ladies,' Demetrius says with a nod. He scoops up our rucksacks and hands them to Alekos on the jetty.

I scramble to my feet and follow Candy. She takes Demetrius' offered hand and steps across the small gap between *Artemis* and dry land.

'Thanks for everything, Demetrius,' I say, as he takes my hand.

'You're welcome.'

I step on to the harbourside and Platia Ammos suddenly feels a lifetime ago. The hum of chatter coming from the multitude of bars and cafés lining the waterfront and the occasional squawk of birds perched on masts is in opposition to the peace and stillness of last night on the beach.

Candy squeezes my shoulder. 'I'll be over there.' She nods to where our rucksacks lean against a wooden post. 'I want to take a couple of photos.'

Demetrius remains on the boat and Alekos walks over to me and takes my hands in his. 'What are your plans for tonight?' We're standing in the same place as we had the first time we'd spoken to him just three days ago, the sun beating down on us even hotter than it had been then. So much has happened and changed in that time.

'We're going to go out to eat and then to Fresko on the harbourside. We love it there – thought it would be a fitting place to spend our last night.' I look up into his hazel eyes. 'If you're not doing anything, maybe we'll see you there? I know Candy and Demetrius aren't exactly on friendly terms right this minute…'

'Don't worry about Demetrius,' Alekos says, letting go of my hands and running his fingers up my arms and down my back until he's holding me around my waist. 'He's what us Greeks call a *milaka*. A friendly insult.'

I laugh. 'Okay, as long as you're sure.'

He leans forward and kisses me. 'See you tonight.'

He lets go and I walk over to Candy. 'Come on, we're seeing them later.'

'Bye, Alekos! *Choi, Demetrius*!' Candy calls without even bothering to look back, her voice dripping with sarcasm.

I can't stop thinking about him. I choose what to wear carefully. Not that I need to impress him. We've gone way beyond that. In the end I borrow Candy's flared white skirt and a canary-yellow linen top with capped sleeves. I love dressing for summer with bare legs and flip-flops – I could get used to this life. Maybe I need to book another holiday in the sun as soon as I get home so I have something to look forward to.

We eat at the same fish restaurant we've been to twice before. I'm getting used to hearing Greek chatter and picking out the occasional familiar word. Our waiter brings out a feast of fried mussels, calamari, prawns with tomato and feta and the biggest Greek salad I've ever seen, yet I long to be back on the beach eating fish from a foil parcel.

As we walk through Fiskardo's winding streets to work off our dinner, I feel glad Candy's skirt has an elasticated waist. It's a sultry evening with little breeze, even when we head back to the harbourside. We find an empty table in Fresko by the water and my heart sinks when I look around and can't see Alekos. What if he doesn't turn up? What if this afternoon on the dock was him saying goodbye, that he's just kinder about ending a one-night stand than Demetrius was with Candy?

Candy flicks through the cocktail menu. 'Ordering a Sex on the Beach is going to take on a whole new meaning for you now.'

I slap her arm yet I can't help but laugh, the knot of tension in my stomach easing as we giggle together. I order a mojito instead.

'Demetrius is an accountant back where they live on the mainland,' Candy says. 'At least that's what I think he was trying to describe to me – a job with numbers, helping people with their money. Can you believe it?'

'I can't imagine either of them anywhere but here, the freedom of setting sail each day. It's a lush life.'

'You're a soppy romantic. I bet it has its downside, everything always does.'

I frown.

'I'm not being pessimistic, it's reality. Like my job – people would kill to be able to say that they're a make-up artist on one of the biggest TV shows in the UK, and I love it, you know I do, but the downside is early mornings and long days. Something's always got to give.'

I gaze across the bay. The lights from the bars reflect on the inky water, sending long zigzag streaks of silver and gold towards the even darker horizon. I don't think I'd ever tire of this view if I was lucky enough to live and work here.

Candy taps the table with her fingernails. 'Look who's just arrived.'

I turn and see Demetrius with Alekos behind him, walking on to the terrace. Relief floods through me and my heart feels as if it knocks against my chest at the sight of him again. He's dressed casually in jeans and a white T-shirt. He catches my eye and smiles. Demetrius is talking to someone and so Alekos walks over alone and pulls up a chair between Candy and me.

'You eat already?'

I nod, but I can barely look at him without my cheeks burning at the thought of us last night, naked on the beach together. I shuffle in my seat, realising I've never been so reckless in my life, not even at university. It's not that I haven't had a one-night stand before, it's just I didn't make them a habit – a one-off with a guy I had at least talked to and seen around before. Last night was on a whole new level.

'I'm so going to miss this,' Candy says to fill my silence. 'Hot lazy days and fabulous food.'

'Life is very different for you back home?' Alekos asks.

'Where do I begin?' Candy laughs. 'No guaranteed sunshine for a start. I'll miss being able to walk to the sea in just a few minutes.'

I stir my cocktail. 'To be fair, we do have good places to eat out though at home.'

'True, but it's not quite the same as this.'

The waitress who served us comes over and smiles at Alekos.

'*Ti kanis*, Aleko?' she says. '*Kala?*'

'*Ola kala.*'

I take a sip of my drink and watch Alekos and the waitress chat, the relaxed way he has, resting back in his chair, his legs splayed around the table leg, his T-shirt hugging his chest. Their Greek is rapid and I have no idea what they're talking about.

'*Ti thelis?*' the waitress asks.

'*Mia biera.*'

'*Kai o Demetrius?*' she nods over to where Demetrius is still talking to the group of men he'd spotted on the way in.

Alekos makes a 'tsk' sound and shrugs. '*Then exero. Meta.*'

The waitress rests her hand on Alekos' shoulder. '*Ta leme argotera.*'

She shoots Candy and me a smile before turning and heading to the bar.

'Do you know everyone on Cephalonia?' Candy asks.

'Not everyone, but a lot. It is island life, you get to know people, even on a big island like Cephalonia.'

'Demetrius has a girlfriend, right, back home?'

Alekos' eyes shift away from Candy's.

She sighs. 'Alekos, seriously, you can tell me, I'm not going to be offended or freak out. I know what me and Demetrius was – a one-night thing and I'm cool with that. I just want to know there's a reason for him being so cold rather than him being just a complete dickhead and using me for sex.'

'There is someone back home.'

'And he's messed about before with other girls, right?'

Alekos shrugs and smiles as the waitress returns and places a beer in front of him. 'He's a grown man. I can't tell him what to do – or not to do.'

'Hey, I understand,' Candy says, glancing over to where

Demetrius is still chatting. 'I'm not exactly squeaky clean myself.'

Alekos frowns and then nods. 'You are with someone too?'

Candy holds her hands up. 'Guilty, but I'll be doing something about that when we get back home.' She grabs her bag off the back of her chair and stands up. 'I'm going to find the ladies.' She raises her eyebrows at me before she weaves her way between the tables and chairs on the terrace.

Alekos takes a sip of his beer. 'You really have no one back home?'

'No one.'

'I'm surprised but happy about that.'

I laugh and stir my cocktail with the straw. 'I've been too busy concentrating on work. I just hadn't met the right person.'

Until now, I want to say, but stop myself thinking it sounds too much. Instead we talk about everything else – work, our hopes, holidays – everything apart from how we feel, what happened last night and past romances.

The bar is packed and filled with laughter and chatter, people eating and drinking. I realise we both finished our drinks ages ago.

'Where's Candy got to?'

Alekos nods towards the direction of the bar. 'Over there.'

I swivel in my chair. Candy's sitting on a stool up at the bar, her tanned legs crossed, a cocktail in her hand, chatting to the guy on the stool next to hers.

'She looks like she enjoys herself,' Alekos says. He stands and reaches for my hand, pulling me to my feet. 'Walk with me.'

Alekos' hand is warm and firm in mine, our fingers entwined as we leave the terrace and walk down to the waterside away from the twinkling lights. The water is black, still and cool, inviting enough for a night-time dip.

'When do you leave Cephalonia and go back home?' I ask as Alekos sits down on the edge of the harbourside, his legs dangling just above the gently lapping water. I sit next to him and he slides his arm around my waist.

'In a week. Demetrius is staying for the rest of the summer then starts a new job in Thessaloniki in September.'

'Does his girlfriend mind him being away for so long?'

Alekos' thumb strokes my side and sends a shiver through me. He looks at me. 'I'm sure she does. She knows what he's like.'

I stare out over the glassy sea towards the pinpricks of light on Ithaca. 'Aren't you going to miss this?'

'Yes,' he says, and I wonder if he means he's going to miss living and working on Cephalonia or miss us, this moment right now, sat side by side sharing this view, our bodies touching.

'It'll be good to see my family. Mama will be happy to have me back. I miss my nephew – he's only ten months old.' He takes his wallet from out of his back pocket and pulls a creased photo out and shows it to me. A baby with big brown eyes, long eyelashes and a shock of dark hair smiles back at me.

'He's gorgeous.'

'So yes, I'll miss this but will be happy to go home.'

It's peaceful here, despite being in sight of the bar with multiple voices drifting towards us mixed with the beat of Greek music playing a couple of bars down. Alekos reaches for my hand and rests it in his lap.

'We have a boat trip booked tomorrow; a family want to go over to Ithaca.'

Life keeps turning and while Alekos will be on board *Artemis* I'll be getting on a plane and heading home. I've never wanted time to stop as much as I do right now.

'If you stayed longer we could have taken you over there. Even quieter beaches on Ithaca, some even more beautiful than Platia Ammos.'

I don't have to look at him to know exactly what he's thinking at the mention of the beach and the time we spent there. His thigh is warm and all I can think about is running my hands over his body and the memory of him pushing me down into the sand, his warm naked body on top of mine.

Alekos cups the side of my face with his hand until I'm looking at him and then he kisses me, lightly at first but with passion as I kiss him back, my arms around him, my hands dipping beneath his T-shirt feeling the heat of his skin.

'Come back to the boat,' he says, resting his forehead against mine, his arms still encircling me.

My head spins, my body dying to say yes and reigniting the feeling from the night before… Despite my head being fuzzy with alcohol, I'm conscious that there's a distance between Candy and Demetrius and obvious regret on Demetrius' part – his intention for a one-night stand only. Somehow it doesn't feel right to go back to the boat tonight, separating from Candy, knowing Demetrius would be sleeping in the cabin next to Alekos'.

'I can't,' I say, ignoring my body screaming yes. 'I can't leave Candy on her own.'

He leans in and kisses me again and for a moment that's all there is – me and Alekos. I don't want our kiss to ever end.

He breaks the spell, pulling away from me. He helps me to my feet and puts his arms around my waist, tugging me to him so our bodies are still pressed together, every muscle firm against mine.

I glance behind him to where Candy is now sitting alone at our table, the man she'd been chatting to at the bar talking to one of the barmen.

'I guess this is goodbye, then,' he says.

I nod. I wish I was like my mum. She'd be back on *Artemis* like a shot, shagging Alekos' brains out, no thought to the awkwardness of leaving a best friend to head back to the hotel on their own, or the fact Demetrius would be able to hear *everything* through the thin cabin walls. But I'm not my mum. I'm not impulsive and rash and I've never been comfortable with random one-night stands, wanting the security of a meaningful relationship rather than the emotional confusion of not knowing how to behave with someone you only know because you've had sex with them.

'I will,' I say, fighting back tears.

If he's disappointed, he's hiding it well. Maybe I really am just another notch on his cabin bed – there will be another girl, another holidaymaker eager and willing to escape the reality of life and have a carefree fling on a beautiful Greek island. Just as Candy was for Demetrius.

He kisses me again and I kiss him back, imprinting his feel, his taste to memory.

'*Kalinikta*,' he says and walks away, shoving his hands in his jeans pockets as he goes. He nods at Demetrius who's still talking to the group of men by the edge of the café terrace and Demetrius glances towards me, then back at Alekos. Does he shrug? I have no idea what he's saying.

Candy hooks her bag across her body and walks over to me. 'Are you crazy?'

My eyes continue to follow Alekos as Demetrius pulls out a packet of cigarettes and Alekos takes one, pausing to light it before they walk along the waterfront towards *Artemis* and away from us.

'I presume he asked you back to the boat?' Candy crosses her arms. 'Why the hell haven't you gone with him?'

'I'm not leaving you to go back to our hotel on your own on our last night.'

'You know I don't mind.'

'That's not the point.'

'Are you sure about this – there's still time to change your mind, go after him. Shag his brains out. Again.'

'*Candy.*' I hook my arm in hers and make my answer clear by walking in the opposite direction to Alekos.

The route along Fiskardo waterfront to our hotel has become so familiar. Walking beneath the archway into the hotel grounds with its swimming pool, palm trees and tubs spilling over with flowers feels like coming home. I don't want to be on a plane tomorrow, heading back to the UK, the reality of real life looming the closer we get to landing.

We walk through the hotel reception in silence, both lost in our own thoughts. One of the receptionists calls out, '*Kalinikta*,' as we go.

I climb the stairs two at a time to the second floor and unlock our bedroom door, closing it behind us.

Candy drops her handbag on her bed and turns to me. 'Are you worried spending another night with him won't live up to last night on the beach?'

I shake my head. 'I don't know. Maybe.' I sit down on my bed and rub my eyes, a lump still in my throat and the feeling of tears threatening to spill. I bite my lip. 'It's a holiday romance that isn't going to go anywhere. How can it?'

Candy goes to the bathroom but pauses before closing the door. She looks right at me. 'Please don't regret this, Sophie.'

Chapter Nine

I wake early and alone in my bed. Candy snores gently, her arms hugging her pillow. It was only yesterday I woke up next to Alekos, our bodies pressed together on the single bed in his cabin on board *Artemis*. I should have said yes; yes to going back with him last night, to recapture the feelings from the night before. Being sensible and putting my friendship first leading me to wake up without him. I wonder if he's awake? I wonder if he dreamt about me last night or will think about me this morning like I'm thinking about him. Tomorrow our lives will be so different, separated by thousands of miles and two different cultures and countries. Today we share memories and the unity of being on the same island at the same time. What were the odds of meeting each other in the first place?

I throw the sheet off, pad across the tiled floor to the bathroom and brush my teeth. I stare at my reflection in the mirror above the sink. Mascara rings my eyes. My hair needs brushing, and it's a deeper red than a few days ago. The freckles across my cheeks have been accentuated by the sun. I close my eyes and reimagine Alekos running his hands across the back of my neck and up into my hair. I remember the smoothness of his voice on the beach when he told me I was beautiful.

My eyes fly open. Get a grip, Sophie. Too much sun, too many cocktails and one night of incredible sex has gone right to my head. I wipe away the mascara, splash my face with cold water and walk barefoot on to the balcony. A woman's already in the pool, swimming lengths, her towel and bag on a sunlounger and an orange juice on the low table next to it. A handful of couples are sitting on the terrace eating breakfast. There are a couple of new faces; lucky people about to start their holiday. I turn away and face the view that had left Candy and me speechless on our first day here. The glass-like sea from the night before has ripples across it and boats dot the hazy horizon. A trickle of sweat begins to creep between my breasts despite the shade of the balcony.

'Did you sleep okay?'

'Uh huh.' I glance behind to where Candy is leaning against the balcony door, her messy blonde hair framing her tanned face.

'You've woken up thinking about him, haven't you?'

The polish on my fingernails has chipped again. I should just remove it and start afresh.

'I can't stop thinking about him,' I say.

'Oh Sophie.' Candy comes over and leans next to me on the balcony rail.

I look at her. 'Am I'm being silly? Being infatuated by a brief holiday romance?'

'No, absolutely not. You two obviously hit it off,' she leans towards me and nudges my arm, 'in more ways than one, but, I don't know, truthfully there's something about you two together, you just connected.'

'You think he likes me as much as I like him?'

'Are you kidding me? Yes, absolutely. He digs you big time.' She puts her hand on my arm. 'Sophie, I saw the way he looked at you.'

The trickle of sweat has reached my belly button and I waft my hand in front of me. I need a cool shower.

'I wish we didn't live so far away.'

'You so should have gone back to the boat with him last night.' Candy turns around to face our room and leans her elbows on the rail. 'A goodbye shag might have done the trick of getting him out of your system.'

'But that's the problem, I don't want him out of my

system.'

'Then stay in touch with him.'

'How?'

'You didn't get his number?' Candy says. 'At least get his number.'

'What's the point?' I stare out over the balcony to the sea stretching towards the distant green-clad hills of Ithaca. 'We're not going to be able to have any kind of relationship with me in the UK and him in Greece. Anyway, I don't want to do the long distance relationship thing. You know how that worked out with James when I went to uni.'

'Then just get his number so if you're still single next year come back here and hook up.'

'He doesn't even live here.'

'It's up to you what you do. It's your life, but just remember it's the things you don't do that you'll regret not the things you do.'

I know she's right. I don't want to get home and regret not at least seeing if he has the same feelings for me as I do for him. A relationship with him would be complicated and difficult but it feels so much more than a holiday romance. Perhaps too much sun and the fact he's hot as hell are clouding my judgement. Yet again I'm confusing lust for love. Why wouldn't I want to hold on to this feeling?

'How long have we got until we have to leave?'

Candy squeals. 'Enough time. Go find him, I'll pack.'

Before I can talk myself out of it, I tie my messy hair in a ponytail, pull on a clean pair of knickers, bra, cropped trousers and a vest top and slip my feet into my flip-flops.

I walk the route from our hotel to the harbour on autopilot, along the paved pedestrian way next to the water and past the shuttered Venetian buildings housing bars and tavernas at the centre of Fiskardo. Whatever happens when I see him now, that first image of him aboard *Artemis* and all those moments we shared together since are mine to keep. I keep telling myself that as I pick up the pace and round the corner to the boats, just in case Alekos isn't interested in staying in touch. Just in case I discover I really am a one-night stand for him.

The second I see the boats I get a sinking feeling. With my heart beating faster I walk closer and realise there's a gap where we'd moored *Artemis* yesterday, just seawater gently slapping the side where the boat should have been.

I put my hands on my hips and take a deep breath, willing myself to not break down in floods of tears. I look around, checking the other boats to make sure *Artemis* hasn't simply been moved, but me willing it and Alekos to be here is futile.

A man with greying hair and a deep tan is repainting the sign on a boat a little further down the jetty. I walk over.

'Excuse me. The boat, *Artemis*?' I shout across.

He looks up from painting and I gesture to where the boat had been.

'Left this morning, early,' he calls back in a strong Greek accent.

I remember Alekos saying last night that they were taking a family out for the day, I assumed it would be at ten, the same time we'd set sail but obviously they'd left much earlier.

'Okay, thank you. *Efharisto.*' I make to go but turn back to the man. 'Do you know when they'll be back?'

He shrugs. '*Then exhero.*'

I take my time walking back to the hotel, regret enveloping me: regret for not going back with Alekos last night, for not telling him how much I like him, for not at least giving him my number, for being too late, for not being able to kiss him one last time.

'That was quick,' Candy calls out as I close our hotel room door behind me. My face must say it all because she takes one look at me and says, 'Oh, he wasn't there, was he?'

I shake my head and let the tears that had been building all the way back stream down my cheeks.

'Oh Sophie, I'm so sorry.' She pulls me into a hug.

I hold on to her. 'I should have gone back with him last night, said a proper goodbye, got his number at least.'

'Sophie, you think too much with your head rather than your heart.'

I let go of her and wipe my tears away with the back of

my hand. Candy's been busy in the short time I was gone, with our suitcases almost packed. I go to the bathroom, gather my wash things and shove them in my wash bag. Red and blotchy eyes stare back at me from the mirror. I sniff and realise there's no choice but to move on, head home and put this week down for what it is – a holiday romance.

'Are you okay?' Candy asks as I walk back into the room and dump my wash bag in my suitcase.

I nod. 'I feel so silly being this emotional over a guy I barely know.'

She squeezes my arm. 'So much for our man-free week.'

Someone else is checking out, so we sit on the armchairs in the airy reception that face the wall of glass that makes up the entrance of the hotel. I clean my sunglasses on the edge of my vest top. Through the windows the purple bougainvillea glow in the sunlight, bright against the pure white of the wall that surrounds the hotel's garden. I glimpse a square of blue through the gate that leads to the waterfront and my thoughts immediately return to Alekos, out there somewhere on *Artemis*, perhaps sailing to a secluded beach on Ithaca that he hadn't had time to take us to.

'*Kalimera*, Sophie, Candy,' Andrina, the lady behind the reception says, pulling me from my daydream. She beckons us over.

We wheel our suitcases to the front desk and I slide our room keys across to her.

'So you are leaving us today.' She takes the keys and taps something into the computer.

'Unfortunately, yes,' I say. 'Thank you for an amazing week.'

She smiles. 'You will have to come back and stay with us again.'

'If we get the chance, absolutely,' Candy says, hooking her rucksack fully on to her back.

'Trust me, we don't want to leave.' I pull the handle of my suitcase up and make to go.

'Hey,' Candy turns back to the desk. 'Would it be okay if

we left our mobile number with you – well, Sophie's number?'

'Of course,' Andrina says.

'Candy, there's no need.'

Andrina looks between us, her smiling face only briefly pinching into a frown. She pushes a notepad and pen towards Candy, who slides it along the marble counter to me.

'Who do you want me to give it to?' Andrina asks.

I scribble down my number and write 'Sophie' above it. 'It's only if someone happens to ask for it, but I'm sure no one is going to.' I hand the notepad back. 'I'm sorry, we're kind of wasting your time.'

'It's just in case a guy called Alekos happens to call the hotel asking after Sophie,' Candy says. 'We know him; he sails one of the boats in the harbour.'

'I understand.' She nods and smiles at me.

My cheeks flush.

'I'm so happy you had a wonderful holiday with us. Have a good journey. *Kalo taxithi.*'

We leave the cool reception and wheel our suitcases out into the heat and sunshine of the hotel grounds.

'That was pointless,' I say, leading the way around the side of the hotel to the small car park at the back.

'You don't know that. You've done everything you can now. What will be will be.'

The journey from Fiskardo in the north all the way to the airport in the south-west of the island is long and has such a different feel to the taxi drive six days ago. I'm lost in my thoughts and Candy seems quite content to remain silent and just concentrate on driving. Every time we get close enough to the coast and catch a glimpse of the Ionian Sea, I wonder if Alekos is sailing by, yet I know the chance of catching sight of *Artemis* are beyond slim. Our lives had entwined for a couple of days and now we've gone our separate ways for good. We were destined to be nothing more than a holiday romance and a sweet memory – Alekos is imprinted on my mind like the imprint our bodies left in the sand.

My heart sinks when we reach the airport, the reality of

returning home getting closer and closer with every moment. We return our hire car and find a trolley to stack our suitcases and hand luggage on. I pull out my passport, boarding pass and mobile and tuck them in the pocket of my cropped trousers.

The minutes tick by, counting down the time we have left on Cephalonia. We check in our suitcases and go through security. We buy a sandwich and an Amita sour cherry juice each and wander around duty free, spraying perfume until our noses are filled with a cloying mixture of rose, sandalwood and musk.

Candy picks up a packet of Kalimata olives. 'Maybe I should get these for my mum and dad? What do you think?'

I put a packet of mountain tea back on the shelf. 'Or you could get a bottle of that sweet red wine we had at the fish restaurant.'

'Is that your phone?'

I realise my trouser pocket is vibrating. I pull my mobile out and look at the screen.

I turn to Candy. 'It's a Greek number.'

'It's him,' she says.

I stare at the number, a lump forming in my throat, my heart beating faster.

'Seriously, Sophie, answer it or I will.'

She reaches towards me and without another thought I press answer and put the phone to my ear.

'Hello?'

'Sophie?'

'Alekos.'

'I didn't think you'd answer. I thought you might be on the plane already.'

'Almost, in another half hour or so. I'm sorry I left without saying goodbye. I should have come back to the boat with you last night, I wanted to... it's just, I don't know, I wasn't thinking straight or maybe it was because I was thinking too much. I tried to see you this morning but you'd already set sail. I want to stay in touch but I know a long distance thing won't be easy... I understand if you...'

'Sophie, Sophie, *sega sega*. Slow down.'

My heart thuds. I've said too much. Maybe he doesn't want a relationship with a woman who lives four hours away by plane. But then he did get my number from the hotel receptionist and why would he do that if he wasn't interested.

'I love you.'

I feel incapable of uttering a word. Candy mouths 'what?' at me.

I shake my head at her, but then smile at the realisation this is exactly what I've wanted to say to him ever since the night on the beach.

'I love you too.'

Candy is practically jumping up and down and fist pumping the air with the olives still clutched in her hand.

'Come live with me,' Alekos says.

Chapter Ten

'I still can't believe you're really going.' Candy closes the front door of her shared house and hooks her arm in mine.

'I'm really going,' I say as we begin to walk down the road. Rush hour has been and gone and our table isn't booked until eight thirty but it's still light out and warm, a sticky July evening without even a hint of a breeze to combat the humidity – my last summer's evening in England.

'I'm envious of you, you know,' Candy says, pushing open the door of our favourite Indian restaurant. 'Finding love like that – I mean how romantic, falling in love with a gorgeous man on a Greek island. It's the stuff of romance novels.'

A waiter shows us to a table in the centre of the restaurant and brings over a bottle of red wine, pouring us a generous glassful each. Two large ceiling fans waft a slight breeze, but it's still sticky in the dimly lit restaurant and I regret not choosing a leafy pub garden for our last night out together. It does hold memories though, this place, our favourite curry house in Bristol where we celebrated Candy's make-up artist job with our friends, and my 24th birthday. My next birthday I'll be celebrating in Greece, with Alekos.

I pick up my glass of wine and knock it against Candy's.

'Cheers,' she says.

'*Yamas*,' I say and grin.

'To you and Alekos.'

I take a sip. 'I'm still missing that sweet wine we had on Cephalonia. I wonder if they have it where Alekos lives?'

'Well, you're going to have such an incredible time finding out.'

The waiter returns with a basket of poppadums and a selection of chutneys and places them between us.

'I'm doing the right thing, aren't I?'

'Seriously, you have to ask?' Candy shoots me a look and breaks a poppadum in half and dips it into the hot lime chutney. 'You couldn't be more in love with him if you tried. I do think you're brave though, leaving everything behind and moving to a new country.'

'Not stupid?'

'Taking a chance on love is not being stupid. Remember, I saw you two together. Yeah he's good looking and sexy as hell so why wouldn't you fall for him, but it was also obvious that you two connected, that there was more between you than just sex.'

I take a bite of poppadum. 'I'm not going to be having curry again any time soon.'

'Ah but think of all that delicious Greek food you're going to be able to have every day.'

'I'm nervous though, about meeting his family.'

'That's kind of natural, isn't it? Meeting your boyfriend's parents for the first time.'

'And living with them.'

'Okay yeah, that's a little more nerve-wracking than the usual "pop over for dinner to meet the parents". They're going to love you, Sophie. I know they will.'

With a stomach full of poppadum, lamb passanda and sag aloo we walk back to Candy's house along a road that I know so well, with the bars, restaurants and shops that I go past five days a week on the bus to work. We reach Candy's front door and it's the moment I've been dreading, saying goodbye.

I take Candy's hands. 'You have to come and visit me and soon.'

'Are you kidding me? The minute I get the chance I'll be on a plane and straight over.'

'It won't be too awkward seeing Demetrius again?'

Candy shrugs. 'I'm sure he's had a string of one-night stands before and can deal with me turning up for a week or two. Don't worry, I won't arrive guns blazing and make his poor sod of a girlfriend aware what a cheating twat her boyfriend is.'

We fall silent and I fight back tears.

'So this is it, tomorrow you're setting off to go and live with Alekos.'

'Yep, but first I've got to take some of my stuff round to Mum's so she can store it for me.'

'You should have asked me,' Candy says.

I shake my head. 'It was an excuse to see her. I can't just up and leave for Greece without saying goodbye.'

'What have you told her?'

'That I'm moving to Greece to live with someone I met while on holiday with you.'

'I bet she's going to have something to say about that.'

'I'm sure she will but there's not a lot she can do about it.'

Candy leans forward and hugs me. 'I'm going to miss you so much.'

I hug her back. 'I'm going to miss you too.'

She pulls back and laughs. 'I'm going to ruin my make-up again.' Tears streak her face and I hand her a tissue.

'You're going to set me off again too.'

'Go be with Alekos, you lucky, lucky lady.' She kisses my cheek, puts the key in her door and unlocks it. With a wave she closes it behind her.

I take a deep breath and set off down the road, wiping away the tears running down my cheeks. Our week on Cephalonia changed my life and it's been a whirlwind since, quitting my job, saying goodbye to colleagues and friends, packing up my belongings and deciding what to take with me to Greece and what to leave behind. My decision to go and live with Alekos has been the biggest of my life and possibly the most reckless. I'm longing to see him again and for him to hold me.

I reach home and turn the key in the lock, checking for any post on my way in. I clatter up the stairs two at a time and unlock the door to the flat. Lucy and Jess aren't home yet; we'd said goodbye the evening before with a bottle of wine and a DVD. I don't know what to do besides have an early night and dream about my new life in Greece that begins once I've said goodbye to Mum.

Chapter Eleven

'Is it because you're pregnant?' Mum asks.

We're standing in her kitchen with two boxes filled with my old stuff between us: school books, paintings, boxing gloves, dungarees, a train-set and Anne Rice novels. It's three hours before my coach leaves for Heathrow and my goodbyes are not going well.

'Is that really the reason you think I'm going to live with him, because I'm pregnant?' I ask.

'Are you?'

'No.'

She pours herself a glass of white wine. 'Sophie, you did only meet him six weeks ago and have only actually spent one week together. What do you expect me to think?'

'Is it too alien a thing for you to comprehend that the reason I'm moving to Greece is because I want to be with him? I love him.'

She takes a sip of her wine. 'Love is a strong word.'

'It's also the right one. Just because you don't believe in love at first sight doesn't mean I don't.'

'Oh, I believe in love at first sight alright, it's what happens after the initial honeymoon period that I'm wary of.'

'I really don't need your negativity right now.' I tape closed the flaps of the box nearest me.

'I thought I'd got rid of all this when you moved out,' she says, scuffing the box with her foot.

'Well, I can't take it with me.' I take a pen from my bag. 'Have you got some paper?'

She points to a used envelope wedged between the coffee and sugar jars.

'This is the address in Greece,' I say, writing it down.

'It doesn't exactly roll off your tongue.' She sets her wine down on the black marbled worktop before pinning the address to the noticeboard next to the door. 'I'm going to make a stir-fry. Do you want some?'

I shake my head.

Her nostrils flare. 'The plane food will taste of plastic.'

I can't help but admire her attempt at mothering. 'Maybe a bit then.'

'The chicken is in the fridge.'

The huge American-style fridge is always full. I take out a cling-filmed plate of chicken breasts, and find bean sprouts, carrots, baby sweet corn and mange tout in the salad compartment. Arms loaded, I turn to see Mum bent over the worktop peeling an onion. Her hair is twisted and pinned in loose curls; the nape of her neck tanned against the soft blonde of her dyed hair. Her vest top is burnt orange, bright against her white gypsy skirt. Despite everything, I want to hug her.

'Have you learnt any Greek yet?' she asks.

I slam the fridge door closed with my foot. 'A little.' I dump the food on the worktop and reach behind the bread bin for a chopping board. Mum chops the onion as if it's a race.

I take the cling film off the chicken. 'Sliced or cubed?'

'Sliced, not too big.'

We stand in silence for a moment, our knives thumping wood.

'So,' Mum says, breaking our rhythm. 'How are you going to get a job out there?'

'Same way as here, apply.'

'Don't be smart. You know what I mean.' She breaks off a

clove of garlic from the bulb and starts peeling it.

'The best place to learn Greek is in Greece. I know I want to start drawing again… I can teach English if I need to. I was thinking of setting up an artists' retreat.'

'You've got high hopes.'

I stop mid-slice. My fingers are sticky with chicken. 'What's wrong with that? I don't want to end up regretting my life.'

Her glossy lips purse. 'I may still have a lot of hopes, Sophie, but I've no regrets.'

'Are you sure about that?'

She drops the naked clove into the garlic press and squeezes. 'You've known this Alekos for less than two months.'

'So what? Because of your lies, I don't know my father at all.'

The garlic press clatters on to the worktop. She reaches for her wine and gulps down half the glass. 'I'll be the first to admit I made a mistake,' she says.

'When have you ever admitted that?' I slap the sliced chicken back on to the plate.

'What do you want me to say?' she asks.

'Nothing.' I turn away from her and wash my hands in the sink. Outside on the patio, the barbeque is filled with ash. Beer bottles look out of place next to the trellis entwined with flowers.

When she finally speaks her voice is steady and controlled. 'I care about you, Sophie, obviously too much.'

'It's not a case of you caring, it's you expecting too much from me – the serious job you've never had. Try sorting your own life out rather than mine.'

She tops up her wine and, marching over to the sink, slams the empty bottle on to the draining board next to me. She used to smell of cigarettes and Oil of Olay, now she smells of onions and the Dior Poison I gave her last Christmas.

'I'm not the one running away,' she says, almost spitting at me. I don't have her sapphire blue eyes. Mine are green, I presume like my father's. I slowly wipe my hands on the towel. I can't even begin to guess the natural colour of Mum's hair she's dyed it so many times. In photos of her when she first had me, all you had to do was take away the dodgy early eighties haircut and clothes, and it was like looking in a mirror.

'I'm not hungry any more,' I say, tucking the towel back on its rail.

'That's typical of you. Go on, avoid the truth. You're throwing away a good job and life here, Sophie.'

'You're so full of shit.' I grab my bag off the worktop.

'What if you don't find the answers you want in Greece?' she asks. She sounds like a soap star, clutching at a cliché for something to say. She follows me down the hallway to the front door. My flip-flops go slap, slap, slap against the polished floorboards.

'I'm not going to find them here.' I unlock the door. We've stood like this so many times before – her standing her ground in her own house, while I escape from her and her folded arms and her big, smothering personality. 'I'll make do with plastic plane food. Enjoy your stir-fry.'

I open the door and a shaft of sunlight creeps into the hallway. Outside, cars glint, even the dirty ones. The tree embedded in the pavement by the front gate has wilted in the heat.

From the shadows of the hallway Mum says, 'If Alekos doesn't work out, you know where I am.'

'Fuck you.' I slam the front door of my childhood home for the last time.

I get back to an empty flat with no housemates to talk to. My old room has been stripped of me. Only faded curtains, a fitted wardrobe and a sheet-less bed remain. Only the red wine stain on the carpet shows I'd even been here. I used to love having the flat to myself on the rare occasions Lucy and

Jess were out at the same time but now I'm desperate for their company as I wander from room to room, at a loss of how to kill the two hours before my coach leaves.

I feel I should phone Mum and smooth things over but I get no further than thinking about it. I want to talk to Candy but after glancing at my watch I realise she'll still be working on set with her mobile switched off.

I make myself a cup of tea, toast a crumpet and sit by the window. I want to tidy, stay busy, but for once the flat is spotless, an ironic leaving present. I wedge the window open, rest my bare feet on the ledge and phone Alekos.

He answers almost instantly. 'Hey Sophie, where are you?'

'At home. I'm ready, all packed, just waiting for the coach.'

His warm, deep voice, caressed by his accent, tickles my ear. 'I can't wait to have you here, Sophie.'

Outside the traffic has snarled up with the beginnings of rush hour. The faintest breath of air filters in through the open sash window. I don't envy them in their cars below, those with their windows wound down, sweating. Different music escapes from car stereos, different tastes and beats clashing. Teenagers in school uniform hang about outside the newsagent opposite, some with ice creams in their hands, others with fags stuck between their lips, their bikes strewn carelessly across the pavement. 'I can't wait to leave,' I reply.

'We're going to meet you at the airport.'

'We?'

'The restaurant's open only in the evening... Mama is excited, she's been cooking all day.'

'I thought it was going to be just you. I don't want to cause any trouble.'

'No trouble,' he says. 'I told my sister and my uncles and aunts they have to wait until home to meet you. I thought everyone there too much.'

He can't see my smile but I hope he hears it. 'I'll see you tomorrow.'

~

71

The deep blue of the sea through the plane window makes my stomach somersault. My legs tense when the plane dips into a descent and I see the coastline spread out, glistening in the sun's glare. I'm dressed for a Greek summer in a new cream-coloured short skirt, thin canvas shoes, a pale blue vest top and no make-up, only a brush of mascara on my eyelashes. I use my sunglasses, wedged on top of my head, to keep my hair out of my eyes.

My Greek phrase book is open in my lap; the words for hello, yes, no, how are you and I don't understand, tumbling around my head, becoming increasingly muddled the closer we get to land. I pull my seatbelt tight and tuck my book and magazine away. Resting my head back against the seat I watched Thessaloniki fill the oval window. Hazy mountains are the backdrop, their muted colours blending with the city in the early morning sunshine. We dip lower, tarmac and parched grass, bright buildings and signs accelerating into view until we screech on to the runway with a jolt.

Emerging from the plane the heat hits me, like the blast of hot air you get in winter when walking into a shop. Heat steams off the tarmac. I'm grateful to leave the sunshine behind and enter the cool building. Luggage endlessly circles in front of me. I don't want to move; I grip the handle of my trolley tight.

Somewhere in here Alekos is waiting. Tucked inside my purse I have the photo Candy took of him on Cephalonia. His lips aren't smiling but his eyes are, shaded from the sun by his hand. His hair is damp and short, his chest tanned and beaded with seawater. In his other hand he holds the octopus that we had cooked over coals, before burning our fingers and tongues eating it.

Sandwiched between a striking woman and beaming bronzed man at the arrivals gate is Alekos, exactly as I remember him. Butterfly wings flutter against my ribcage. He grins, dimples puncturing his rough cheeks. His hand shoots up in a wave and the three of them step forward to greet me.

I'm in Alekos' arms, head buried in his neck, my lips

tasting the salt on his skin, his lips kissing my forehead, my cheeks. If I'm aware of his parents watching, I don't care. This is the start of my new life – of our new life together.

Alekos pulls away from me. 'Sophie, this is my mother, Despina, and my father, Takis.'

Takis is a well-worn version of Alekos, as tall as him and lean. Despina is something else: vivid and memorable, her red top as loud as her. She grasps my hands and kisses me on both cheeks. 'Welcome!'

Takis steps towards me and plants another two kisses on my cheeks. '*Ti kanis?*' he asks loudly. '*Kala?*'

I reply with a nod, hoping a nod is the right thing to do.

There is no respite from the heat outside. It's early July and the air smoulders. Alekos puts his arm around my waist and I hold on to him all the way to the car. I can't stop looking at him or smiling. His skin is darker in the sunshine and mine is like white chocolate against him. Despina leads the way with Takis manoeuvring a trolley with my bags on it through the car park. He turns round and smiles at us at least five times between arrivals and the car, while Despina talks constantly at us. I don't understand a word.

I stand with Despina as Takis and Alekos argue, I assume good-naturedly, over how best to put my luggage in the boot. Despina keeps clicking her tongue disapprovingly and commenting. She looks at me and flashes a red-lipstick smile. She reaches forward, touches my hair and nods. '*Parre poli oreo,*' she says.

I continue to smile.

'Very lovely. *Kokkino,*' she says, pointing to my hair, and then after realising I still don't understand, points towards her lips.

'Red!' I say, nodding.

'Bravo, Sophie!'

The boot slams shut and Alekos turns to us. 'Let's go.'

Expensive clothes shops line Thessaloniki's pavements and

amongst them I glimpse familiar names of *Accessorize*, *Virgin* and to my disbelief good old *Marks and Spencer* as we beep and swerve through packed streets. Sweat pools into the small of my back and I feel a trickle slide down the side of my face. The car's air conditioning is working flat out but that does nothing to combat the summer sun penetrating the back windscreen. Alekos holds my hand, his thumb rhythmically rubbing up and down mine. The streets are a patchwork of shade with strips of sunlight fighting their way between the tall apartment blocks that make up the heart of the city.

Alekos leans towards me as I gaze out of the window. He points to cream buildings overlooking a square filled with people with a glimpse of sea beyond. 'The docks are over there,' he gestures somewhere in front of us. He wrinkles his nose. 'We're not going that way.' He squeezes my hand. 'You okay?'

My other hand clutches the back of Takis' seat. Every time we turn a corner, Alekos and I, belt-less in the back, fall against each other. I nod.

'You can shower at home, sleep if you want,' he says. 'Before everyone comes over.'

'Everyone?'

'To eat. You'll love it, we have a feast prepared.'

The apartments thin out the further we go away from the centre. The traffic doesn't though and I grip Takis' seat tighter as cars, including ours, veer erratically between lanes on the dual carriageway.

'*Thes nero*, Sophie?' Despina turns to me and asks. 'Want water?'

'Do you want a drink?' Alekos says. 'We can stop here.'

I shrug. 'I don't mind.'

We screech to a halt at the side of the road, double-parking alongside another car. Takis switches off the engine and the air conditioning stills. The car rapidly becomes as effective as a night storage heater.

'*Psomi, kapoozi, nero ke* Coca Cola!' Despina shouts after Takis. He disappears inside what looks like a grocer's and reappears seconds later beckoning to Alekos. I take my phrase book from my bag as Alekos gets out and use it to fan myself.

'*Ehi zeste*,' Despina says, imitating me flapping the pages of my book with her hand.

I feel sweat snaking down the centre of my back. I sit upright away from the seat and stay very still. Takis appears from the shadows of the shop with a blue carrier bag, while Alekos carries a watermelon in both arms.

'Like *kapoozi*?' Despina asks.

I take *kapoozi* to mean watermelon and nod. 'Yes. *Ne*,' I answer, correcting myself.

She beams at me as Takis starts the engine and Alekos struggles on to the back seat.

For the rest of the journey I sit with my head resting on Alekos' shoulder, my hand on top of the *kapoozi* between us and let their rapid words wash over me. Maybe I'll soak up the language like a sponge. I want to do more than just nod and smile but I'm content for the time being to simply head to my new home.

Alekos nudges me awake from where I doze, rocking against his shoulder, my arm still encircling the cool, green skin of the *kapoozi*.

'Home,' he whispers. His breath tickles my ear.

'I didn't mean to fall asleep,' I say, rubbing my eyes. The glare from the sun distorts my view. All I can see of my new home is a silhouette. The car slows between open gates and crunches over gravel. Takis parks neatly in the shadow of the restaurant next to two other cars.

'What you think?' Alekos asks. I scramble out of the car after him. I shade my eyes with my hand and savour the elegance of the building with its arched windows, red-tiled roof and pale, caramel-stained walls.

'I had no idea it was this beautiful,' I say.

Alekos grins and hooks his arm around my waist, pulling me towards him until I'm pressed against his chest. 'Are you happy?'

'Happy doesn't even come close,' I say. His eyebrows scrunch in confusion. I kiss him. 'I'm so happy I met you.'

He has changed me. He's made me question what I want, what life means. He has dragged me out of the 9 to 5 rut. There is no normality about this place. *Estiatorio O Kipos* the sign above the restaurant entrance reads. Alekos says it means *The Garden Restaurant*. To me it means a new life.

Takis drags my luggage from the boot. Despina has disappeared inside and I hear her calling to someone. Alekos smiles and beckons me towards the garden and sunshine.

Beyond the terrace there is a bar with the same red roof and warm-coloured walls as the restaurant. Olive trees line the far edge of the garden, their intricately woven branches shading the seating below. I imagine couples getting cosy beneath the trees once darkness descends. The garden's centrepiece is a fountain encircled by a wooden bench. The place is so quiet I can hear the trickle of water.

I've swapped housemates for Alekos and his family, a flat above an off-licence for a bedroom above a first-class restaurant, a kitchen windowsill of ailing spider plants for a garden the size of a football pitch, and noise and traffic for fields that merge with the sky.

'*Aleko, pes tin Sophie gia tin dulia*,' Despina calls from the restaurant steps.

'*Ochi tora, Mama.*'

I look at him. 'What is it?'

'*Tipota.* Nothing.'

'Go on, tell me.'

He shrugs and points. 'See the bar?'

I nod.

'That's where you are going to work.'

'I'm going to what?'

'It's decided. You won't have to find a job. Mama thought it'd be easy for you.'

'I don't know enough Greek – any Greek yet.'

'Don't worry, you won't be alone.'

He catches my hand in his. I stare across the garden, trying to imagine myself behind the wooden bar, taking orders, pouring drinks, talking Greek and looking out on a patio of strange faces.

'Here is very different to England. We have waiter service, there won't be anyone at the bar,' he says softly. He turns my face towards his. 'I've said too much. I don't want to worry you.'

'I'm not. It's a lot to take in.' I pull away from him. I can feel the nerves I've been battling against build in my stomach. I take a deep breath. 'I was going to sort myself out.'

'I know. I told Mama...'

'Sophie!' Despina's voice pierces the air.

A shorter, darker and younger version of Despina appears next to her on the steps with a baby clamped to her hip. She clatters towards us, her free hand held open. She plants kisses on my cheeks.

'I'm Lena, Alekos' sister,' she says. 'This is Yannis, my...' She turns to Alekos. '*Pos lene yios?*'

'Son.'

'My son.'

'He's gorgeous,' I say.

'Christo? Eleni?' Despina shouts into the shadowy restaurant. '*Ela edho!*'

I hold on to Alekos tighter. 'My aunt and uncle,' he says. 'They came early to finish making food. Everyone wants to meet you.'

Takis' rough hand squeezes my shoulder. '*Endaksi, Sophia?*' he asks.

I nod and realise I understood something. I am okay.

I lose count of how many times I'm kissed before we go inside, and even then I'm bombarded with questions, which are interpreted by Alekos, and made to try all sorts of food before Despina ushers me upstairs for a well-needed shower and a moment's quiet to adjust.

I wash away the grime of travel. Wrapped in a towel, I stick my head out of the bathroom door before nipping across the empty hallway. The air conditioning is on in our bedroom. Our bedroom. It sounds so strange, yet the thought makes me smile. I bounce across the room, my smile breaking into laughter I can't contain. My wet hair slaps against my shoulders and water trickles down my back. I drop the towel on the floor where I stand and let the cool air caress my bare skin. The balcony windows are wide, the curtains open, but I don't care. The sky is hazy and the bright white paintwork of the balcony shimmers. The bedroom door scrapes open and then closes with a click. Alekos whistles under his breath. His warm hands on my skin replace cool air, one hand on my stomach, the other sliding between my breasts. He nuzzles my neck, his stubble rubbing, scratching, his lips tickling, kissing.

'I like you living here very much,' he says. His hands smooth across my skin. He presses into me. His belt buckle digs into the small of my back.

'There are no neighbours,' I say.

'No. But they fruit pick. They see you.'

We make love on our bed, in our room. It's like the first time on Cephalonia again, discovering each other; the weight of his body on top, the tautness of his muscles and the warmth of him inside me as we move slowly and silently together. He is my second skin and I want to know every part of him. He leaves me sleeping and I wake up alone. I hear him downstairs, confidently talking in Greek, an Alekos I will grow to know. I'm not sure how long I've slept for, but I feel refreshed, lying naked on top of the sheets. The sun has moved across the sky, stretching a block of sunshine further across the wall. Slowly, I pull myself on to my elbows. The early haziness has dispersed and for the first time I see Mount Olympus, clear and magnificent. My new life in Greece has begun.

More Books by Kate Frost

Contemporary Women's Fiction

The Butterfly Storm
The Butterfly Storm picks up from where *Mine to Keep* ends, following Sophie to Greece where the reality of life in another country, living with her boyfriend's parents puts a strain on her relationship with Alekos. When her estranged mum is involved in an accident, it's the perfect excuse for Sophie to escape back to the UK to reassess her life and who she loves.

The Birdsong Promise
The sequel to *The Butterfly Storm* is due to be released in autumn 2018.

Beneath the Apple Blossom
The first book in *The Hopeful Years* series.
The emotional trauma of IVF, the strain of friendships and relationships surviving the toughest of times. The lives of Pippa, Connie, Sienna and Georgie interlink through infertility and infidelity, friendship and betrayal, love and loss, as they risk everything to achieve their hopes and dreams.

The Baobab Beach Retreat
The second book in *The Hopeful Years* series.
When Connie leaves behind a cheating husband in the UK for her aunt's beach retreat in Tanzania, the last thing she wants is for her life to once again be complicated by men. Yet her time to heal is short-lived and a reckless decision shatters her hopes for a fresh start. Can Connie put the past to rest and find peace and love in a country far from home?

Children's/Middle Grade Fiction

Time Shifters: Into the Past
An exciting time travel adventure for 9-12 year-olds.
When Maisie is time-shifted to 1471 during a school trip to
Warwick Castle, it's the beginning of an adventure bigger than
she could ever have dreamed of. The only problem is she has
to share it with Lizzie, the class bully, instead of her best
friend Danny, who has got caught up with the army heading
to the Battle of Barnet. The chase is on to find Danny and a
way home before being lost in time forever.

Time Shifters: A Long Way From Home
The second book in the *Time Shifters* trilogy is due to be
released in winter 2018.

Time Shifters: Out of Time
The final book in the trilogy is due to be released in winter
2019.

Thank You To...

Firstly, huge thanks to my writer friends, Elaine Jeremiah, AnnMarie Wyncoll and Judith van Dijkhuizen for their thoughts and suggestions on how to make a relatively early draft of *Mine to Keep* stronger. Judith in particular your comments throughout the manuscript were invaluable and there's no way I'm publishing any future books without you taking a look first! My editor and proof reader, Helen Baggott, was dependable and thorough and gave the manuscript its final polish.

Once again my fabulous cover designer, Jessica Bell, came up with a cover that not only captured the feel and tone of *Mine to Keep* beautifully (and made me want to be lounging on a Greek beach instead of being in rainy England dealing with a tired and temperamental three year-old), but tied it in perfectly with *The Butterfly Storm*, the book that continues Sophie's story.

Like my novel *Beneath the Apple Blossom*, *Mine to Keep* was mainly written and edited during the two mornings my son attends nursery and when my lovely parents look after him on Tuesday afternoons – it's amazing how having limited time seems to enable more to be done than having all the time in the world... Now my son is (finally!) sleeping better I have more time in the evenings when I actually feel awake enough to write – so thank you Leo for that! As always my husband, Nik, along with my parents, have been as supportive and as encouraging as ever.

Author's Note

Thank you for taking the time to read *Mine to Keep*. If you enjoyed this book, please join my mailing list to be the first to find out about my future book releases. To sign up simply go to www.kate-frost.co.uk, click on 'Fiction Newsletter' and enter your email address. Subscribers will receive occasional news from me about new books, special offers and my writing life.

If you liked *Mine to Keep*, please consider leaving a review on Amazon and/or Goodreads, or recommending it to friends. It will be much appreciated! Reader reviews are essential for authors to gain visibility and entice new readers.

You can find out more about me and my writing at www.kate-frost.co.uk, or follow me on Twitter @Kactus77, or on Facebook at www.facebook.com/katefrostauthor.

Printed in Great Britain
by Amazon

29128832R00054